"Would you co[nsider] marrying me?"

Nicholas Redfern's voice was deliberate as usual.

"You're . . . you can't be serious," Jenny stuttered at last. "We agreed that we'd both been put off matrimony."

"That's what prompts my suggestion. My personal likes and dislikes must give way to the fact that I must find a wife. A nominal marriage isn't much to offer, but it might just appeal to a woman who is no more anxious than I am to get emotionally entangled. We already know we work well together. Perhaps we could also live together happily. Does it sound preposterous?"

"I don't know how it sounds," she confessed. "I'll have to think about it. A marriage in name only?"

"Yes, unless we both decided differently . . ." Jenny could have sworn the smile suddenly crossing his face contained a certain arrogant confidence.

Sally Stewart, an English author, spent her childhood with four older brothers in wartime London, a noisy but invaluable experience. After schooldays in Kent and university in London, she began a long career with *Reader's Digest*, which involved much organizational work and travel abroad, but no writing. Home, now, is with her husband in an old country town in the Thames Valley, and work centers around Oxford. Entering and unexpectedly winning a magazine competition led to her present addiction to writing—an addiction she says is one of the more pleasant to have.

Love upon the Wind

Sally Stewart

Harlequin Books

TORONTO • NEW YORK • LONDON
AMSTERDAM • PARIS • SYDNEY • HAMBURG
STOCKHOLM • ATHENS • TOKYO • MILAN

Original hardcover edition published in 1987
by Mills & Boon Limited

ISBN 0-373-02862-8

Harlequin Romance first edition September 1987

CHAPTER ONE

JENNY normally stopped outside the house in Hans Place for an admiring glance, so perfectly did it combine the solid worth required of a respected firm of family solicitors with just the right amount of trendy elegance to prove that it had also moved with the times. Today, though, she decided to admire the premises of Redfern, Redfern & Fox from within, wanting to escape from a blizzard that had almost worked the miracle of clearing Knightsbridge of lunchtime crowds.

She dived through the doorway, saw too late a large figure bearing down on her from the opposite direction, and cannoned into it with a force that left her dizzy. She expected to ricochet off on to the floor, but was caught instead by arms that encircled her suddenly like steel bands. Steadied and back on her feet again, she wasn't immediately released. Helplessness invaded her like an incoming tide, making her despise herself and also making her enraged with a man who probably knew exactly how she was feeling. Office gossip credited him with a reputation that lay somewhere between Bluebeard and Don Juan; Jenny thought it was probably exaggerated, but not by much. He had the battle-scarred looks and sardonic charm that women seemed to find irresistible; combined with a stormy marriage and an even stormier divorce, they made him both exciting and available. She'd gone out of her way since joining the firm to make it clear that she wasn't in the queue of dazzled women

waiting to be noticed, but the fear that she might be
suspected of having flung herself into his arms
deliberately now made her glare at him like an
outraged duchess being manhandled by the groom.

'Fire somewhere, Miss Bartlett?' he enquired. 'You
came through the door like a cannon-ball.'

'I was in a hurry to get indoors . . . sorry if I inflicted
any damage.'

He inspected her slight frame thoughtfully. 'Difficult, I'd say. In any case don't apologise, it was an
unexpected pleasure. You normally avoid me like the
plague.'

He was not only too observant by half, but also
maliciously aware of having disconcerted her for the
second time in the space of a minute.

'Nothing personal about that,' she assured him
sweetly after a moment's thought. 'It's just that I've
forsworn all men, having been seduced by a handsome
villain at a tender age.'

'Pity!' Because he regretted her fate worse than
death, or her subsequent seclusion? She didn't know,
but it wasn't the moment to enquire. He'd been on the
point of leaving the house in a hurry, and she'd
bandied words with him long enough.

'I'm afraid you'll have difficulty finding a taxi—it's
pretty foul out there,' she told him helpfully.

Another considering stare seemed to suggest that he
was in no hurry after all. 'We must take the rough with
the smooth, Miss Bartlett, and I'm enjoying the effect
of snowflakes in your hair.'

No doubt about it; the man had a genius for
unsettling her, damn him. Natural skill in making
women aware of him had been honed by practice into
a fine art. She managed a cool smile and retreated
from the contest, making a mental vow to avoid him

even more completely in future.

In the office she shared with Gwen Marriot she brushed snow off the petals of the crimson polyanthus she'd brought in with her and put it on the windowsill. It had emerged from her brush with Nicholas Redfern more undisturbed than she had. Fortunately the sight of it distracted her room-mate from noticing her flushed face.

'What's that supposed to be ... the promise of spring?'

The jaundiced question was typical, and made Jenny grin naturally again.

'It's to keep us going in what my paper this morning describes as the worst January in living memory. Admit that it cheers the place up!'

'What you really mean is that you couldn't bring yourself to walk past that old rogue who sells them outside the tube station. I expect you overpaid him as usual and told him to keep the change.'

'I can resist him,' Jenny mumbled, 'it's that dog of his—it's got such a reproachful eye.'

'Specially trained to spot mugs like you,' said Gwen. The acid comment made her feel quite cheerful, and she relented to the extent of smiling at her colleague. 'Like to bet James won't come in next with a sprig of white heather pressed on him by some so-called gypsy?'

But it wasn't James Redfern, senior member of the firm, who came in next. Instead, Andrew Fox, nephew of a Fox now retired, put his fair head round the door and grinned at them. Something in his hand, under its wrapping of soggy paper, looked suspiciously like another polyanthus. Gwen, who worked for him, stared at it, fascinated.

'I don't believe it. Not you, too. Couldn't you look a

poor sad dog in the eye either?'

'I didn't even notice the dog,' Andrew confessed. 'I was rather taken with the girl standing in for the old boy at the flower stall. She must have been damned near freezing to death, but that didn't stop her smiling at me. I asked her if she happened to be called Eliza.'

'And she replied "Not on yer life, 'enry 'iggins," I suppose,' suggested Jenny.

'Well . . . words to that effect.' Andrew smiled at the memory of an encounter he'd obviously enjoyed. He was a man who liked people, and whose eye for a girl was unerring. Especially, he liked Jenny Bartlett, but in the six months she'd worked for Redfern's he had to admit that he'd made very little progress. She no longer looked haunted, as she had when she'd first arrived. Her mouth smiled easily now, and she was gentle and friendly as a lamb. That wasn't all there was to Jenny Bartlett, he felt sure, but it was all there was on view. One day he was going to find the woman beneath that calm, efficient exterior. For the moment, though, a few other problems required his attention. He looked sternly at his hand-maiden and beckoned her to the door.

'Come with me, Gwendoline. We have work to do. Nicholas threw a brute of a brief on my desk just after lunch, as if I didn't have enough to do. Said he was on his way to court, by the way; poor old Harrington's case is being heard this afternoon.'

Jenny nodded, hoping that Mr Harrington's lawyer would have managed to arrive on time. Almost certainly he would. Other people might search snowy streets in vain for a taxi, be turned away from fashionably crowded restaurants, or arrive at a theatre to find that it was full. Not Nicholas Redfern. It was what she most disliked about him, that air of infallible success, still intact surprisingly after his ruined marriage. She didn't blame the woman who'd found him impossible to live with, but Gwen had snubbed her thoroughly one day for saying so. Miss Marriot was prepared to write off most of the human race without a second thought, but such affection as she had to offer was given to Nicholas. She referred to his ex-wife in terms that would have made a sailor blush, and rejoiced in the miracle that such a beautiful, amoral bitch hadn't quite managed to destroy him.

Since then Jenny had kept her opinion about him to herself. He wasn't destroyed, but he was certainly damaged. She recognised the fact because she was damaged herself. Broken hearts didn't get a mention in medical textbooks, but the condition existed. Hearts mended after a fashion, but thereafter their owners tended to hide them out of harm's way. Her own recipe for avoiding future disaster was to keep men firmly at arm's length; his was to offer women everything but the heart's affection, and enjoy the antics they engaged in to catch his attention. It was true that she avoided him like the plague, but it hadn't ever occurred to her that he might notice. The strange idea that her aloofness might have hurt him held her suspended for a moment, then she swatted it from her mind like an intrusive fly, and finally got down to tackling the load of dictation given to her that morning by James Redfern. She worked steadily for the rest of the afternoon, unaware that the early winter darkness was closing in outside, or that Gwen was getting ready to leave.

'You staying all night, by any chance?,' Miss Marriot enquired on her way to the door.

'No . . . but James wanted this to go tonight. I've almost done.' She spared a hand from her typewriter

to wave goodnight, then went hammering on again.
Ten minutes later she walked into her boss's room
with the completed contract and put the accompany-
ing letter in front of him to sign.

'Sorry, Jenny, my dear . . . I've made you late, and
it's a filthy night!' He sounded so concerned that she
was tempted to pat his head, bald as it was except for a
fringe of silver hair that made him look like a worldly,
benevolent friar. He was the kindest man she'd ever
met, and the steadiest. She'd been a ghost-driven
wreck when she first began to work for him six months
before. He'd made no attempt to probe her trouble,
and gently insisted that she was there to work and
concentrate on what she was doing, not peer over her
shoulder at happiness left behind. But he was kind as
well, and his often generous praise was intended, she
knew, not for an efficient secretary but for a girl who
was slowly hauling herself out of an agonising period
of her life. They carefully observed their working
relationship, but shared affection sweetened the days
for both of them.

James signed the papers, then beamed as a thought
struck him. 'Andrew's still next door. He can give you
a lift home.'

'He *can*, but he might not relish being asked to go
north when he lives due west of here! Don't worry
about me . . . I shall slosh my way to the underground
as usual.'

She smiled good night, but when she let herself out
of the front door ten minutes later it was to find
Andrew on her heels.

'James says you require looking after,' he said
happily. 'I'm just the man for the job.'

Jenny smiled but shook her head. He would expect
to be invited in at the end of the ride to Bayswater. She

didn't mind sharing her supper with him, but she wasn't going to share her bed as well, and Andrew was a man who took it for granted that one thing led to another.

'Kind of you both to think about me, but I'm used to looking after myself. In fact, I'm incurably independent ... cussed, my darling grandfather used to say!'

'You're a mystery,' he answered unexpectedly. 'One of these days I'm going to unravel it.'

His hands imprisoned her, making it impossible to walk away.

'There's no mystery,' she said after a moment. 'I'm just a cat who likes to walk by herself. Anyway, it's much too cold to stand here analysing my not very interesting psyche!'

'That's exactly what I mean. Give most women the chance to talk about themselves and it wouldn't matter how cold it was. But you go dancing away the moment anyone tries to get near you.'

'Well, I'm certainly going to dance away now ...' She stopped speaking because a taxi drew up at the kerb in front of them and the long limbs of Nicholas Redfern unfolded themselves from the back of it. She wished fleetingly that Andrew's hands were not still clamped round her shoulders.

'Do I interrupt a tender good night?' Mr Redfern's voice had its usual undercurrent of mockery, but she thought his face under the harsh light of the street lamp looked drawn and tired.

'How did it go this afternoon?' asked Andrew, releasing her at last.

'Badly,' said Nicholas briefly. 'Harrington's such a fool in the witness box. Our only hope is that the jury won't have the heart to convict him. He *looks* so damned guilty they may decide, rightly, that he's innocent.' Nicholas frowned at the darkened windows behind them. 'You're not the last to leave, I hope? I particularly asked Angela to wait for me.'

'She went half an hour ago . . . it *is* half past six, you know,' Jenny pointed out.

'Damn and blast her eyes . . . I *told* the girl I'd need her when I got back. If I could remember where she lives I'd go and haul her back again.'

It was on the tip of Jenny's tongue to remind him that 'the girl' was his secretary, not his personal slave, but something in the strained face watching her made her say something she certainly hadn't intended.

'Is there something I can do?'

'Rash, Miss Bartlett! But I'd be eternally grateful if you'd send a long telex to New York for me. I must have the answer before court re-opens tomorrow morning.'

He dismissed Andrew with a brief good night, and unlocked the front door. It took him ten minutes to draft the message he wanted to send. Then, while she began to transmit it, he went upstairs to warn James that noises coming from the office didn't mean the house had been invaded by burglars. He didn't hurry back, and Jenny approved of a consideration she hadn't expected. It was much easier to work with him not standing at her shoulder, and steady fingers were needed for transmitting an important message that mustn't be garbled. She was watching the reply printing itself on the machine in front of her when Nicholas came back into the room. There was a final little spurt of words, then she tore the paper out of the machine and handed it to him. A long sigh of relief told her that he'd got the answer he needed. He folded the paper neatly and put it in his pocket, and the release of tension in him lit his face with a smile she had never seen before. She grinned back, warm with the knowledge that Mr Harrington's fate now looked less uncertain.

'You're white with fatigue—or is it hunger?' Nicholas asked suddenly.

'Bit of both, I expect—lunch was rather sketchy today.' She went to pick up the coat she'd thrown down, but his movements, for a large man, were always quick, and he got to it before her.

'I'm sorry about the fatigue, but the hunger I can possibly do something about. We'll see if there's anything to eat upstairs.' Jenny opened her mouth to say that she'd rather go home to eat, but closed it again, aware that she'd be talking to an empty room. Mr Redfern was already on his way up the stairs, and her coat was going with him. She followed in his wake, fuming at a piece of high-handedness that was typical of him. They passed the door to James's flat on the second floor, which she was familiar with, and went on climbing to the attics above, where Nicholas had his private lair. Droppers-in were not encouraged, and even Andrew never went up there except by invitation. She realised that the telex message had been very important indeed to affect him to the extent of letting down his drawbridge. Doors on the landing obviously led to bedrooms out of sight, but the room she was ushered into ran almost the whole depth of the house under the rafters. A wall of bookcases at one end screened off the kitchen. The books helped to humanise the room, and hugely squashy armchairs looked comfortable, even though she suspected that they weren't; she liked somewhere to rest her head. But though it was clever and fashionable, she had the impression that it was the work of a professional decorator, offering no clue to the personality of the man who lived there. Nicholas poured dry sherry for them both, without bothering to ask whether that was what she would like. She saw the grin that touched his mouth, and distrusted it.

'It's supposed to be the lady's line, about slipping into something casual! But grant me five minutes to get out of this damned suit!'

Jenny took a heartening swallow of sherry, telling herself firmly that the situation wasn't running away with her. She prowled along the bookshelves, thinking they might tell her something that the rest of the room withheld. His choice was almost too catholic to tell her anything at all . . . Trollope and Henry James rubbed shoulders with Dick Francis and Simenon in the original French; there was a lot of biography and travel, which she would have expected, and nothing to surprise her until she came to a shelf of poetry. Even more unexpected was the fact that it was clearly read, because here and there slips of paper marked passages he might want to find again. She was looking at one of them—a love poem by Robert Graves—when Nicholas came back into the room. He was now dressed in shabby corduroy slacks and a polo-necked sweater, and looked bigger than ever. The informal clothes made a stranger of a man she only knew in the dark, elegant suits of a top-flight lawyer. She was briefly aware of wishing there'd been time to do something to her own face and hair, then was so annoyed with herself for the thought that she sat on the edge of a chair staring indifferently into space. The less she said, the sooner he would get bored with her and let her go home.

'Shall we view the possibilities in the larder?' he enquired, amused by an attitude that told him to take nothing for granted. By now, every other woman he

was acquainted with would have been trying to make
him aware of her, not the reverse. Jenny Bartlett
obviously despised feminine tricks, and something in
her considering gaze suggested that she also despised
him. It was a piece of impudence he'd like to make her
pay for, or at least repent of.

He beckoned her into the kitchen and opened the
fridge door.

'Eggs, bacon, butter and bread. Basic, but better
than nothing. We could always pretend we'd just got
out of bed and it was breakfast-time!'

She took no notice of the murmured suggestion and
carefully refused to catch his eye. Instead, she
rummaged in a vegetable rack and pulled out onions,
peppers, and some tired-looking tomatoes.

'The makings of piperade ... will that do?' she
asked coolly.

'If I knew what it was, I'm sure I'd say yes. But I
didn't bring you up here to start working again.'

'I enjoy cooking ... and in any case I'm going to
make you do some of the work.'

She thought he looked slightly taken aback and
swallowed an inward smile at the reason—Mr
Nicholas Redfern wasn't used to having the control of
a situation taken out of his hands. But she had to be
either bossy, or mesmerised by him, and he wasn't to
know that in a kitchen she felt happily on home
ground. He was given the peppers to de-seed and chop
while she dealt with the rest of the ingredients, but the
expression on his face told her that he was wishing
they'd settled for fried bacon and eggs. He opened a
bottle of fine Chablis, obviously hoping that good
wine would help to redeem an embarrassing situation,
then gingerly tackled the plate that she put in front of
him. She watched this performance, trying to stifle the

laughter bubbling inside her, tried to turn it into a cough and failed as he laid down his fork and stared at her.

'Now come clean, Miss Bartlett. I'm sure I remember my father saying that you live alone. How do you come to be such an inspired cook?'

Jenny smiled at him over the top of her wine glass. 'Not everyone who lives alone exists on a diet of boiled eggs and fish fingers.'

'You're begging the question. Enlighten me.'

She wondered why all her colleagues suddenly seemed hell-bent on taking her apart. First Andrew, now this man, who would be much less easy to fob off.

'Well, it's true that I live alone, but I don't find that a reason not to enjoy the food I have to eat. In fact, I grew up thinking that if I wasn't going to be the creator of some stupendously beautiful garden—a new Gertrude Jekyll—I'd like to be a great chef. That didn't happen, but I'm happiest when I'm cooking.'

'Redfern's have reason to be grateful you didn't follow either ambition, but why didn't you?'

Jenny glanced up to find his dark eyes studying her across the table. The initiative had somehow slipped away from her and he was in charge again. His question had been gently put, but not out of idle curiosity. For this moment, at least, he wanted to know what made Jenny Bartlett tick.

'My grandmother talked me out of those ambitions,' she said at last, choosing her words slowly. 'I was eleven when my parents were killed and she and Gramps took me in. If I'd said I wanted to be a trapeze artist he wouldn't have turned a hair, but my grandmother was made of more conventional stuff. She said I could cook and dig to my heart's content when I had a home of my own; till then I'd better apply myself to a more normal career. So I read languages at Cambridge where we lived . . . took a secretarial course as well, and finally came to London.'

As a life story it was brief, and there were gaps in it she clearly didn't intend to fill. He knew that she was twenty-five . . . more than old enough to have found that home of her own with some man or other and, looking at her, it was hard to believe she hadn't been offered one.

'The grandparents . . . are they still in Cambridge?'

'They died within a few weeks of one another . . . soon after I came to London,' said Jenny with difficulty. 'I loved them dearly . . . still miss them.'

She didn't elaborate on that either, but he was aware of a sadness too hurtful to be talked about. It explained some, but perhaps not all, of the solitariness that clung to her.

'You hadn't joined Redfern's then, I think,' he said merely. She shook her head, remembering the terrible days of her first job in London; shattered by losing Luke and desperately lonely in a city that seemed inhumanly indifferent to her unhappiness, the death of her grandmother and Gramps had been the last, almost unbearable grief. She'd been near drowning in a sea of self-pity when James Redfern pulled her ashore. Nicholas watched her face, aware that her thoughts were far away. There was time to notice how thin and delicately boned she was—not obviously beautiful, but the man would be a fool who didn't take a second glance. Her hair had the colour and shine of a horse-chestnut, and clear hazel eyes were beautifully set under brows darker than her hair. Everything about her was simple to the point of austerity . . . no overheated womanish clutter, and yet she gave an impression of femininity. As a connoisseur, Nicholas approved the intriguing contradiction.

'I rather destroyed your evening,' he said suddenly, thinking it was time to remind her that he was there. 'What would you have done, left to your own devices?'

'Cooked supper for myself, and listened to a broadcast concert. It was going to be a good one,' she added regretfully 'Ashkenazy playing Rachmaninov.'

'It's not quite the same thing I know, but remind me to play you the record some time.'

The expression on her face prompted his next question. 'Why the surprise? Like most people, I own a record-player and a library of records.'

'I suppose Rachmaninov's the surprise. I'd have guessed Brahms or Sibelius thundering out, or Bach's Brandenburg concertos if you were feeling intellectual!'

His sudden shout of laughter was another surprise in this altogether unusual evening. She was remembering, too, that shelf of poetry, when he reached over and took her hand. Confused by the knowledge that things were going much too fast for her, she was towed across the room to an armchair by the fire.

'You're right as far as you go,' he agreed blandly, 'but I can also cater for the times when I'm not feeling intellectual. What shall it be, Miss Bartlett . . . the love duet from *Butterfly*?'

She knew that he knew as well as she did how the first act ended. It was difficult to sound unconcerned when her heart seemed to be jumping into her throat, but she made a brave attempt at it.

'Another time, perhaps . . . fatigue *is* catching up with me, and you must be very tired yourself.'

She was thankful to have clutched at something reasonable that needn't provoke him into proving that it wasn't. A tête-à-tête evening with Nicholas Redfern had, she was beginning to think, the same dangerous qualities as a walk through a minefield. 'Please don't think you have to drive me home,' she said firmly. 'I can get a taxi outside the door at this time of night.'

To her great relief he didn't argue. He merely took her downstairs, put her in a taxi, and, as she afterwards discovered, pre-paid the driver.

'Thank you for your help, Miss Bartlett, and for the piperade ... it's been an interesting evening.'

His face, seen in the light of the street lamp, looked so serious that just for a moment she was tempted to think he meant what he said. Then she remembered who it was standing there ... not a sensitive, amusing and altogether charming man, but the all-conquering Nicholas Redfern, caught at a moment when he was feeling tired and slightly grateful.

CHAPTER TWO

IT was another grey January morning—the sort that held out little hope of daylight arriving before darkness closed in again. Jenny breakfasted in the alcove she called her kitchen, watching sleet spatter on the skylight above her head, and wondered why she didn't feel like crawling back into bed until spring arrived. What she felt, in fact, was more alive than for a long time past . . . like a drowsy hedgehog suddenly tempted to shake off her coverlet of leaves and investigate the world again—Mrs Tiggywinkle herself, awake after a long snooze! She grinned at the ridiculous idea and set off for the underground, buoyant in a way that she found exciting but odd. Nothing had changed since yesterday . . . she was still a tiny, lonely drop in London's ocean, and no fairy godmother could restore to her the people she had loved and lost. All the same, she smiled at the tired-faced girl strap-hanging alongside her and saw her smile back; cheerfulness kept breaking in.

She bought an extravagant armful of daffodils at the flower stall, smuggled the biscuits she'd brought with her to her mournful friend, and walked into the office telling herself that there was no need to mention the events of the previous evening to Gwen. An hour later she was in James's room when the door was thrust open and Nicholas Redfern walked in. No corduroy trousers and sweater this morning . . . he was formal in dark grey flannel again. The apology for interrupting them was brief, and so was the 'Good morning, Miss

Bartlett,' he just remembered to offer her. But his eye lingered on the daffodils on his father's desk, and she felt deflated by the small cynical lift of a dark eyebrow. Nothing *had* changed. This suavely inimical man could never have chopped vegetables for her at a kitchen table; she'd fallen asleep during that long session at the telex machine and dreamed the whole thing. When the door had closed behind him again James didn't seem in a hurry to return to the letter he'd been in the middle of dictating.

'I gather my son pressed you into service yesterday evening.' His eyes twinkled over the lawyer's regulation half-moon spectacles. 'He wasn't fit to be heard this morning on the subject of a secretary who not unnaturally chooses to go home at the end of her working day!'

'He *had* warned her, I gather, and it was rather crucial,' Jenny pointed out, wondering why she felt obliged to make excuses for a man who never saw the slightest need to make them for anybody else.

'So I understand,' agreed James placidly. He didn't pursue the subject, but the hint of a smile lingering in his eyes suggested that Nicholas might also have mentioned how the evening ended. She got back to her own room to find Gwen Marriot shaking a disapproving finger at her.

'Holding out on me, you snake! What's this I hear about late-night sessions over the telex machine? Andrew told me you got hijacked on the doorstep.'

Jenny let out a pained sigh. 'A hotbed of gossip . . . it's a wonder any work gets done at all. I'm sorry to disappoint you, but it was nothing to get excited about—a message that needed to be sent last night, with an answer back straight away. I don't think Angela could have understood how important it was.'

'She understands now,' Gwen said with relish. 'I gather that our Mr Redfern wasn't minded to mince his words with her this morning. Nor is Angela . . . an "impossible bastard" is the very least of what she could lay her tongue to! If you want my opinion, she'll stay for as long as it takes to find herself another job, unless she's invited to go before then.'

'Well, if she does go, the obvious solution is for *you* to change jobs,' suggested Jenny. 'Nobody would find it hard to work for Andrew, and you'd be more than a match for Nicholas Redfern. Let's face it—no one else is that we're likely to find. Angela's right: he *is* impossible!'

'Led—not driven—he's a lamb.' Gwen blushed under her room-mate's disbelieving eye, but didn't retract the opinion. 'It's true, so you can stop staring at me as if I'm ripe for a lunatic asylum. You've just got to know how to handle him.'

'I think there's about as much chance of handling a full-grown tiger. But if you've got the knack of it we could avoid four more secretaries disappearing within the next six months.'

'It's not as simple as that,' Gwen said regretfully. 'It needs an old dragon like me to keep Andrew's nose to the grindstone and I'm not decorative enough for Nicholas—he wants beauty as well as brains.'

'He wants more than he deserves . . . don't we all?' she added hastily, because the tart little comment made Gwen stare at her. She could see her room-mate's fertile mind beginning to imagine some steamy seduction scene played out over the telex machine the night before; Heaven send she never learned about the supper together upstairs that followed it. That *would* give her something to work on!

The rest of the cold, wet day was depressingly

normal, and the ritual retyping of Admiral Greenaway's will—the fifth to her knowledge—was reason enough to feel bored. She told herself that it would be a relief to get home, but the prospect of a solitary supper and a book she'd been wanting to read suddenly didn't look very exciting. It made her smile more warmly than usual when Andrew sauntered out of his own room to perch himself on the end of her desk.

'A proposition, Miss Bartlett,' he suggested with a grin.

'Tell me more,' Jenny said cautiously.

'Come with me to a gala at Covent Garden on Friday. The full works . . . Royalty present. Can you possibly resist it?'

'Why me, and not your current girlfriend?'

'There's a slight coolness between us at the moment. In a fit of pique, Emily has accepted an invitation to the same event from someone else. You normally refuse all my lures, but this time I hoped I could appeal to your kind heart. I need a beautiful girl Emily can't recognise; then she can spend the evening wondering whether she's tried me too far!'

'It sounds a bit unkind,' mused Jenny thoughtfully.

'Only to someone as nice as you. Come—do,' he begged. 'Leaving Emily aside, it's bound to be quite an evening . . . full fig, and all our decorations to be worn.'

Perhaps it had something to do with a lift of her heart that had come and gone too soon. She heard herself suddenly and surprisingly give in. 'I can't guarantee to give Emily anything to worry about, but I'd love to see the gala. Thank you, Andrew.'

She went home thinking she'd been foolish. Loneliness was a state she'd painfully got used to; it would be madness now to start needing other people again. She needn't have accepted for Andrew's sake—there were probably a dozen girls he could have taken instead. She'd just been carried away by the thought of an evening's excitement, and by last night's discovery that a man's company was a pleasure she was starved of. Damn Nicholas Redfern for reminding her of the fact!

There was also a more immediate problem. Nothing in her wardrobe was going to grace a Royal gala, much less knock Emily's eye out. She sloshed her way, muttering, through lunchtime puddles next day and went back to the office broke but confident that at least she wouldn't let Andrew down. Her first buy had been a long velvet skirt of chestnut brown. What came next was almost as expensive, but too beautiful to be resisted—a ruffled silk shirt the delicate glowing colour of dry sherry. A sash of coral satin and matching sandals, brought the outfit to life.

By the time Andrew came to collect her on Friday evening Jenny had got as far as admitting to herself that she was glad to be going out. Her ruinously expensive clothes hadn't been bought in vain, and perhaps Emily would have something to worry about after all. Andrew's approving eye confirmed the fact. He was used to seeing her minimally made-up, dressed in the rather severe clothes she wore to the office. In full fig, as he'd requested, she rather took his breath away.

'Jenny, my sweet, you're gorgeous,' he announced, more seriously than she normally heard him speak. 'My loved one can't fail to be chewing her fingernails!'

'A few hundred other people will be present . . . she may never see us at all.'

'She'll see us all right,' he predicted, and in this he

turned out to be quite right.

Jenny was aware of the precise moment when a red-haired girl, becomingly falling out of a black taffeta dress, turned round and spotted them. She flashed a smile at Andrew, and a distinctly measuring glance at his companion, then turned back to the man at her side.

'Bernard Cavendish, of all people,' Andrew noticed joyously. 'That pompous bore on top of the ballet, which she doesn't enjoy anyway. Was there anything more delightful!'

Jenny shook her head at such unseemly crowing, then saw his expression change. 'Good Lord! I know everyone who's anyone's here tonight; still, I didn't expect our revered partner to sit through this sort of thing!' She followed the direction of his gaze and found herself staring at the frowning face of Nicholas Redfern. In the formal black and white of evening dress, which he wore without the self-consciousness of most men, he was a devastatingly attractive menace to be avoided. She wiped from her mind the memory of a charming man in shabby corduroys and sweater, and offered the briefest of smiles in reply to his nod. She only had time to notice that he was with an oddly matched group of friends before a rustle of excitement running through the foyer announced the arrival of the Royal couple. Her own glimpse of them lasted a bare ten seconds, but the fact that they were there at all infected dancers and audience alike with some extra-special sparkle.

At the end of an enchanting first half of the programme Andrew guided her through the crowd filling the Crush Bar to where the drinks he'd ordered beforehand were waiting. It seemed sheer perversity on the part of Fate that they should find themselves immediately next to Nicholas and his friends. Judging by an expression that he was doing his best to make affable, Jenny decided that he shared Emily's opinion about the ballet. She thought the probability was that he'd smile and ignore them. Not at all—they were greeted with a warmth that even surprised Andrew, and introduced to a couple who were identified as Sir Arthur and Lady Ainslie, and their daughter Joanne.

Sir Arthur, a small, broad power-house, of a man whose energy seemed ill-suited by evening clothes, wrung her hand in a grip that made her wince, and invited Andrew and his companion to join them for supper after the performance. It wasn't at all what Mr Fox had had in mind, but he hesitated for a fraction of a second too long, hunting for an excuse. It was assumed that they would go, and she couldn't help noticing that Nicholas Redfern suddenly looked remarkably pleased with himself.

'Sorry about that,' Andrew muttered as they made their way back to the auditorium. 'Can't think why I was so damned slow.'

Jenny recalled Miss Ainslie to mind—a pocket Venus whose tightly-fitting gown of white and silver sequins had left almost nothing to the imagination. 'Nor I,' she agreed tranquilly, 'although she did rather fill the eye!'

'Didn't she just! Not my type, though; I like elusively beautiful girls that require pursuing.'

It was lightly said, but she had a moment's suspicion that she'd been intended to take him seriously. Perhaps a large supper party was a good thing after all. 'Pound to a penny he'll take us to the Savoy,' Andrew grunted beside her next.

'Tough!' His grin answered her, and they settled down to watch the scarlet curtains of the Opera House loop up and swing apart. The gala wound its way to a glittering finale, there were flowers, cheers, and curtseys of incomparable grace directed at the Royal Box, then suddenly it was over. Jenny put her hand in Andrew's for a moment.

'Unforgettable ... I can't thank you enough for bringing me.'

Her face was illuminated, and he was tempted to kiss her there and then in the middle of the auditorium.

He turned out to be right about the Savoy, and the pair of them walked in, doing their best to stifle a fit of giggles. Nicholas Redfern watched them approach, hand in hand, thinking that he suddenly felt a hundred years old. Evening dress suited Andrew's fairness, and the girl by his side was transfigured with happiness. Whatever had happened to her in Cambridge must have been desperate if this was how she should normally look.

It was an odd but interesting supper party. Their host monopolised Nicholas, and Miss Ainslie promptly threw herself at Andrew, which left Jenny to make Mary Ainslie feel that she wasn't an uninvited guest at her own party. She didn't exactly help a stranger; all Jenny had to go on was the outward sign of her husband's success coupled with inward glimpses of a self-deprecation that amounted to despair. Lady Ainslie was expensively dressed and her once-beautiful, now faded hair, was a tribute to the hairdresser's art. Still the total effect was one of dowdy disheartenment. It was hard going trying to draw her out, and Jenny had almost given up when a lucky reference to a recipe that hadn't worked suddenly turned a key. The sad face next to her broke into a smile and the failure was diagnosed with the utmost certainty. 'Too much fat in the mixture—makes it heavy,' she pronounced firmly. Jenny agreed, and from then on they didn't look back. Mary Ainslie loved to cook, but one of the crosses she had to bear was that a rich man's wife wasn't expected to bake her own bread. Jenny realised compassionately that the poor woman still hadn't discovered what it was that she *was* expected to do.

The background music in the restaurant was discreet enough to be ignored but Joanne had no intention of doing so. The moment she'd finished her Aylesbury duckling she instructed her father to stop talking to Nicholas because she wished to dance with him. Andrew seized his own opportunity and stood up to take Jenny on to the floor.

'It's a rum party, wouldn't you say?' she asked ruefully.

'Yes, I would, but for the next few minutes we're going to forget it. God bless the Savoy . . . nice, old-fashioned smoochy music.'

His arms pulled her close and she felt his cheek nestle against her hair. It occurred to her that he was either a more practised philanderer than she'd thought or the much-advertised affair with Emily was a blind. While she was still considering this another couple drifted by—Joanne, apparently welded to Nicholas Redfern. They all returned to their table; Nicholas politely steered Mary Ainslie round the floor and Andrew chanced his arm with the pocket Venus. Jenny made laboured conversation with her host, grateful for the fact that Nicholas and his partner were soon back. She'd had time to realise that it would be her turn next, and was ready for a question which he hardly bothered to make sound like a question at all.

'Shall we dance, Miss Bartlett?'

'I think not,' she said gently. 'I'm very out of practice and I think I've had more than enough excitement for one evening.'

'Chickening out . . . or did Andrew rush you a little?'

'He was the perfect partner.' She stressed the pronoun ever so slightly, leaving in the air between them the merest suggestion that it wasn't how she would consider *him*. The truth was that her heart failed her at the thought of being held in his arms. A single life was lonely but bearable as long as your body didn't know what it was missing. Andrew had been the perfect partner simply because, sweet and kind though he was, her bones and blood were unaffected by him. Instinct told her that wasn't how it would be with this man.

He accepted the refusal with such indifference that she wondered why he'd bothered to ask her at all, and then allowed himself to be collared by Sir Arthur again. An evening that had become rather tedious finally dragged itself to an end. They stood in the foyer saying goodbye, and Andrew, attention momentarily distracted, let himself be out-manoeuvred. He'd parked his car a stone's throw from the Savoy on their way to Covent Garden. In that case, Nicholas suggested, why did he not drop the Ainslies off in Mount Street, which was directly on his way home? A taxi could take Miss Bartlett to Bayswater and himself on to Hans Place. It would have been discourteous to refuse in the watching face of Mary Ainslie. Andrew smiled at her, and threw his colleague a glance that warned of revenge in store. On the whole Jenny didn't object to the arrangement, though she realised it would have been all the same if she had. It might have been hard to persuade Andrew that the evening ended when he left her at Bayswater, whereas Nicholas Redfern probably couldn't wait to be rid of her.

Little was said during the short taxi ride and she made a point of staring determinedly out of the window.

'I liked your rig this evening,' he said suddenly, running a finger along the velvet fold of her skirt lying on the seat between them. 'Very . . . fetching.'

It was deliberate . . . his usual game, in fact, of amusing himself by disconcerting her.

'Hardly to be compared with Miss Ainslie's, though,' she pointed out sweetly. 'I expected to see you return from the dance floor looking like a Pearly King!'

With perfect timing, the taxi stopped at her front door. Jenny leapt out, but found Nicholas following her across the pavement. He took the key out of her hand, but didn't hurry to unlock the door for her.

'Andrew told me once something that I now realise is true.'

Whatever she'd expected him to say, it certainly wasn't that!

'He said there was much more to Jenny Bartlett than met the eye. I agree with him, but I'm also wondering what there is that meets the mouth!'

There was no time to answer, evade, or dash through the door. His mouth covered her own, gently at first, then suddenly not gently at all. She held out against him for a moment or two, but resistance didn't stand a chance. Delight was surging through her body like a rip-tide, washing away every careful defence pieced together since Cambridge days. When Nicholas finally let go of her she was too shattered to notice that he was breathing hard and not making a very good job of smiling carelessly.

'The mouth's full of surprises, too! You'd better go inside, I think, before I'm tempted to do some more research.'

She stumbled through the door he opened for her and fled up the stairs, without stopping to notice that he started to walk away and had to be reminded by an ironic toot that a long-suffering taxi driver was still waiting to take him home.

CHAPTER THREE

A GIRL had never been more grateful for the certain fact that Saturday and Sunday had to intervene before she was obliged to face Monday again. Two whole days might be enough to put her shattered self together again. Winter had relented suddenly and a comparatively mild Sunday tempted Jenny to go looking in the secret places of Kensington Gardens where she knew the first crocuses might be found. It was too early in the year for visitors, and she had the green spaces almost entirely to herself, apart from a handful of people being towed behind their dogs. Her heart lifted even at this small escape from bricks and mortar. Nothing would turn her into a true Londoner, and one of these days the problem of where to go next would have to be grappled with if she wasn't to spend the rest of her life in a two-roomed flat in Bayswater. Redfern's had provided a haven when she needed it most, but she was repaired again now and strong enough to refloat herself somewhere else. After Friday evening the idea was insistent in her mind that she must do it soon. A goodnight kiss was scarcely something to turn into a drama—it was the conventional way to end any evening that stopped at a girl's front door. She was certain that was how Nicholas regarded it. But a few hours in his company had cracked her little shell wide open. A newly-hatched duckling blinking in the light of day couldn't have felt more exposed than she did now. The word made her wince inwardly—expose her was exactly what that destructive kiss had done.

She went into the office on Monday morning, cool and apparently confident again. Gwen, there before her, was struggling to complete her crossword as usual before Andrew came in and finished it for her.

'How did Friday evening go?' she asked, busily writing in 'Odin' for 'The god of love and discord.'

'Lovely,' Jenny answered casually. 'Marvellous programme, and of course all the beautiful people were there . . . including our Mr Redfern.' If she didn't mention the fact, sure as fate Gwen would find out—put two and two together and make six. As it was, surprise made Miss Marriot blind to the fact that Jenny's face had gone slightly pink.

'Nicholas at the ballet? My God! He's an opera buff usually, and very rude about preening caper-merchants . . . male *danseurs* to you and me!'

'He was being taken,' Jenny explained, 'guest of some people called Ainslie and their dazzling blonde bombshell of a daughter.'

'Oh well, that explains it, of course.'

Satisfied that she could now account for this strange deviation from Mr Redfern's norm, Gwen was ready to let the subject rest, but Andrew chose this moment to walk in, advanced on Jenny and inspected her face with a hand held under her chin.

'Has she got measles, or something?' enquired Gwen.

'I'm trying to discover how much of a pass Nicholas made at her. The swine snitched my girl and left me to cart his friends home.' Aware that two pairs of eyes were now fastened on her, Jenny knew that a great effort was called for. 'I wasn't raped on the doorstep, so there's no need for you both to get excited. A brotherly peck—that was the extent of the pass,' she reported unblushingly.

Andrew hooted with joy. 'He's slipping! The poor old lad is definitely past it.'

Too late, the expression on Gwen's face made him swing round to see Nicholas standing in the open doorway. Mr Redfern's comprehensive glance took in Gwen and Jenny pink with the effort of trying not to laugh, and Andrew still congratulating himself that honours were now even.

'Get home all right?' Nicholas asked blandly. 'I forgot to mention that Ainslie's not only a J.P., but obsessive about careless driving by those who have wine taken. He's even been known to shop his own nephew before now.'

The sight of Andrew's face was too much for them. The girls exploded into helpless laughter, and by the time they'd sobered up both men had disappeared and the day's work had finally begun. She saw no more of Nicholas during the day and only learned over a sandwich lunch with his secretary that his resemblance to a bear with a sore head was even stronger than usual.

'Don't know why I stay to be insulted,' Angela muttered. 'All you can say for the man is that life is never dull when he's around . . . not quite the same as working for old James!'

'I happen to like working for him,' said Jenny truthfully.

She remembered that conversation sitting in her boss's room after lunch, waiting while he made up his mind about the outpourings in front of him of some temporarily demented client. It was what she loved him for most—his feeling of responsibility for people more muddled than himself. He was like a G.P. of times past, helping people in trouble by listening to them before he tried to solve their problems. James Redfern looked up suddenly and smiled to have caught her staring at him.

'You were looking very solemn,' he told her.

'Thinking great thoughts!'

'Can't put my finger on it, but you look not only solemn but different as well. You're over-thin, Jenny. Do we work you too hard?'

She shook her head, still off balance emotionally and inclined to burst into tears at the kindness in his voice.

'I'm afraid there's no question that Nicholas works too hard,' James said suddenly. 'I know he's got the constitution of an ox, but he worries me all the same. He's fallen into the old trap, of course—used work as an anodyne for unhappiness and got hooked on the pain-killer instead.'

Jenny mumbled something about a very full life, hoping James would now get back to work. But he hadn't quite finished with the subject.

'Ought to have a wife again, and children. I'd like to be a grandfather while I can still enjoy it, not when I'm in my dotage.'

'Well, you're a little way off that yet,' she pointed out cheerfully. He looked so regretful that she hoped he never heard Gwen's opinion about his son. *She* was certain that Nicholas had been choked off matrimony for good. Women flung themselves in his way, and he probably didn't sleep alone upstairs unless he chose to, but she couldn't see him risking marriage again; he wasn't a man to make the same mistake twice. Jenny led James gently back to the work in hand again and the rest of her day was peaceful and, as Angela had predicted, rather dull.

Listening to a broadcast concert that evening, she was reminded of another one that she'd been made to miss. Nicholas had gone through the motions then of suggesting that he'd play her the Ashkenazy recording, but motions had been all they were; the invitation to share a musical evening wouldn't come.

Something else came instead, a week later. One afternoon when she happened to be in the office by herself Nicholas walked in and dumbfounded her by an invitation to dine with him. 'There's a catch from your point of view,' he confessed with the smile that now and then transformed his harsh features.

'You mean I have to cook the dinner?'

She hadn't meant it seriously and was taken aback to see him suddenly look thoughtful.

'It hadn't occurred to me, but now that you've brought it up, it's a marvellous idea! I had the impression that you didn't exactly take to Arthur Ainslie, but you seemed to be getting on well with shy Mary, and very few people do.'

At least, Jenny thought, she now knew the reason for the invitation; it wasn't that Mr Redfern yearned for her company. She'd have liked to ask why such an unlikely couple were his friends, but those were not the sort of terms on which she stood with him.

'I'm obliged to return their hospitality, and there's a man I'd like Ainslie to meet, but Mary hates what she thinks of as 'smart' restaurants. Could you really manage dinner for six without killing yourself?' He sounded so doubtful that she smiled at him.

'It doesn't sound very difficult, if James will give me the afternoon off.'

He nodded and walked away, and she was left to assume that the arrangement was on. By the end of the afternoon, mind wandering from the work in hand, she'd planned and discarded half a dozen possible menus and given no thought at all to an evening immediately ahead with Andrew. When the day of the dinner party came, she said goodbye to James at lunchtime, and told Gwen merely that she'd got the afternoon off. Let Nicholas be more talkative if he felt inclined. She'd been told to buy whatever she thought fit, and to consider the flat her own. Dolly Parkes, the lady who'd been 'doing' the house for the Redferns since time immemorial, would get a room ready for her and she needn't think of traipsing back to Bayswater. Jenny had nodded and not committed herself. How simple it would be for the host to assume that his hostess was expecting him to finish the night with her. Only, not this hostess.

She did her shopping and took it back to Hans Place, confident that Nicholas wouldn't bother her. Told that she was capable of producing a meal he wouldn't be ashamed of, he would take her at her word, and only tear her to shreds the following day if she let him down. By mid-afternoon a carbonnade of beef was waiting to go into the oven, richly brown, and suitably nutty in flavour. It would need only a topping of French bread softened in garlic butter and put in the oven to turn golden-brown when the time came. The first course—cream cheese blended with beef consommé, sherry, and a hint of curry powder—was already setting in the fridge; she had only to finish off a tarte Tatin, praying that the upside-down apple pie would allow itself to be turned out perfectly, and then settle down with one of Mr Redfern's books until it was time to change out of her working skirt and sweater.

Nicholas was so late getting back that she'd begun to imagine the dinner-party would take place without

him. He looked tired, and anxious until he took in the
peaceful room, full of the scent of jonquils and some
other delectable smell drifting in from the kitchen,
and Jenny dressed in a long patchwork skirt and a top
of pale cream cashmere.

'I'd apologise for being late, except that it so
obviously doesn't matter,' he said, smiling at her. 'Tell
me what I need to open in the way of wine, then I'll go
and take a much-needed shower. Something delicate
or hearty?'

'Both,' she said promptly. 'Delicate white, and
hearty red.'

'It shall be done . . . and thank God for a woman
who knows her own mind.'

He reappeared just as a ring at the doorbell
announced the first pair of guests downstairs—not the
Ainslies, but a couple Nicholas introduced as Oliver
and Freda Wheatley. Jenny saw all the more forcibly
why she'd been required for Mary Ainslie's sake.
There would surely be no common ground between
Mrs Wheatley's diamond gloss and a woman she
remembered as being both diffident and dowdy.
Oliver Wheatley was in keeping with his wife—
languid, elegant, and maliciously witty. What could
have possessed Nicholas to entertain two such couples
together?

She discovered the reason in the course of the
evening. Oliver was an architect of swiftly rising
fame; Arthur Ainslie's current venture was a holiday
complex to be built on the site of an abandoned village
in the Tuscan hills north of Florence. Nicholas was the
mutual friend introducing them to each other. He was
also, Jenny had to admit, a superlatively good host,
welding together by sheer deliberate charm people
who would normally have had nothing to say to one

another. Further acquaintance with Sir Arthur Ainslie didn't convince Jenny that she liked him; he was abrasive, opinionated, and barely courteous to a wife whose own self-confidence hadn't survived twenty-five years of being married to him. Aware that their opinions would differ on almost every subject under the sun, Jenny did her best to steer clear of him, but when they were disposed about the room after dinner, drinking coffee and brandy, he appealed to her directly about the Venetian watercolour hanging over the fireplace. It was delicate and beautiful, depicting a wraith of a city emerging from a sea shot with the opalescent colours of dawn.

'Namby-pamby thing,' said Sir Arthur, with all the assurance of a man who couldn't tell a Constable from a Picasso. 'Nicholas ought to get himself a decent oil painting—don't you agree, Miss Bartlett?'

'No,' she said baldly. 'I happen to like water colours, and I can't think of anything more suitable for painting Venice.'

A twitch of Nicholas's dark eyebrow told her that he was listening to the conversation.

'You're very definite, I must say,' Ainslie commented. 'What else do you do, besides look very decorative, and lay down the law about art?'

'Oh, I cook the dinner occasionally,' said Jenny, grateful to find that Oliver Wheatley was hovering beside her.

'You mean, you cooked it tonight?' She almost began to feel sorry for the man. He didn't know what to make of a girl who didn't sound or look like any cook he knew, who wasn't Nicholas's wife, nor his mistress, either, as far as he knew. Mr Wheatley, practised operator, was just as tiring to deal with in his way, and Jenny was grateful when the long evening

came to an end. By the time Nicholas had returned
from shepherding his guests downstairs, she'd stacked
things neatly in the kitchen for Dolly to deal with in
the morning. He walked into the sitting room with the
air of a man who'd exerted himself for others and now
could please himself. She thought he looked danger-
ously relaxed and confident.

'Well done, Jenny wren! Not the easiest of
evenings, but a success, thanks entirely to you.'

She registered the fact that 'Miss Bartlett' had
disappeared. It was a warning sign, and the glint in his
eye was an even surer one.

'I think we deserve another glass of brandy,'
Nicholas said next.

'Not for me, thanks . . . I'm just about to go home.'

'Nonsense . . . you're staying here. It's nearly one
a.m., and you've been working since nine o'clock this
morning.'

'I'm tired,' she acknowledged desperately, 'but I'm
going home.'

There was a little silence in the room, in which she
imagined that the thumping of her heart could be
clearly heard. Nicholas stared at her for a moment,
then poured out the brandy he'd offered himself.

'As Arthur said, you're very definite! I've never
known a girl make it so crystal clear that she didn't
trust my intentions. My inclination, Jenny wren,
would be to take you to bed, but if you said no you
could sleep here without fear of being touched.' His
voice was very quiet, but she had the impression of
having angered him. She would have liked to say that
it was herself she distrusted, but that would have been
to give too much away.

'I didn't intend to wound,' she heard herself say
instead.

Nicholas smiled at her suddenly, making her feel that she was forgiven. 'You certainly succeeded in needling Arthur more than he's used to!'

'Is he used to anything but getting his own way?'

'Probably not. His way is usually so much better than anyone else's.' Jenny's sceptical expression nettled him. 'It's true . . . the man's a genius in his own way, tied to a woman he's left far behind but never tried to offload.'

'Better for her if he had,' she answered obstinately. 'She's three parts destroyed . . . is she supposed to be grateful for that?'

'Come now, you're being ridiculous. You make her sound like the victim of some Victorian melodrama. Mary Ainslie's a nice, tedious woman—not entirely happy, perhaps, but making her own choice about staying with a life of luxury. Don't blame it all on him.'

'I do blame him,' Jenny flung at him, stung by the male condescension in Nicholas's voice. 'She's mesmerised by him . . . don't you see it in her face when she looks at him? That's why the poor creature stays; not for wealth she doesn't know what to do with. That's how women like Mary Ainslie are . . . constant! She's an object-lesson to the rest of us, never to put our happiness in the hands of a man.'

She regretted the words as soon as they were out, but it was too late.

'Is that how you've escaped disaster . . . unlike the rest of us?' The bitter query was thrown at her like hailstones, dredged up out of his own past unhappiness. 'Miss Bartlett safely walled up in her ivory tower, out of harm's way?'

'Miss Bartlett didn't manage things quite as well as that,' she confessed slowly, because the desire to have him understand overrode for the first time the dread of talking about her own failure. 'I did what most women do ... put my happiness completely in one man's hands. He wasn't free and it nearly broke my grandparents' hearts when I decided to live with him. Gramps was a canon ... the gentlest man who ever lived, but with standards of his own that were never compromised. Luke's divorce eventually came through and I waited for him to say when we'd be married. It took me two months to discover that his second wife wasn't going to be me, but someone I'd imagined was my friend. That's when I ran away to London. Gramps died soon afterwards, and my grandmother soon after that. She just gave up without him.'

Jenny stopped speaking, unaware that her face was wet with tears until Nicholas walked towards her and gently mopped her cheeks with his handkerchief.

'I'm sorry, Jenny wren. You gave me a rough outline once before, and I thought you were joking.'

'I meant you to at the time,' she told him. 'I'd got wary of people knowing by then—especially men. All my Cambridge acquaintances seemed to take it for granted that I'd be ready to leap into bed with *them* once Luke had gone.'

'I can imagine,' Nicholas agreed sombrely. He understood now something about that goodnight kiss after the Savoy party that had surprised him at the time. 'No wonder you put me in my place a little while ago! We *both* seem to have come unstuck in our choice of partners ... mine turned life into a battlefield, yours made it a wasteground. No inducement for either of us to try again.'

Poor James, Jenny thought sadly; it looked certain that he was going to have to make do with not being a grandfather at all. They'd come a long way from the subject of the Ainslies that had started the argument, but they'd ended up having discovered some common ground. Nicholas put down his glass and said, in a voice that brooked no refusal, that this time he was going to drive her home.

CHAPTER FOUR

THERE was no pricking in her thumbs a couple of mornings later to warn her that life was on the point of changing gear. Signs of spring were beginning to appear even in London for anyone who bothered to notice them, but Jenny certainly wasn't expecting any personal excitement. She came back from lunch in time to see Gwen coming out of James's room, but there wasn't anything odd about that. The two of them were old friends and enjoyed an occasional chat together. Still, Miss Marriot's normally deadpan face did hint at some change in the air.

'Angela's walked out,' she announced briefly. 'I thought it was on the cards, but that sort of unprofessional behaviour lets us all down.'

'Maybe . . . but I've no doubt the provocation was great,' Jenny replied. 'Where do we go from here?'

'*You* go to James's room. He wants to see you.'

Shorthand book and pencil in hand, Jenny walked along the hall to her boss's room. It looked just as usual . . . the day's clean sheet of paper in the blotter in front of him already heavily doodled over, the hideous clock on the mantelpiece ticking as loudly as ever. James threatened at least once a month to throw it away but never did so. It had been there since his grandfather started Redfern's, and she doubted whether even Nicholas would be able to bring himself to get rid of it when the time came. She sat listening to it, waiting for James to start work. He seemed in no hurry and it took a long time to frame the sentence that finally came out.

'Jenny ... what would you say to a change—working for Nicholas?'

Had her heart actually stopped beating? No, now it was working overtime, pumping blood round her body at an alarming rate. Perhaps she was suffering from palpitations, temporary madness? His eyes, kind and steady as always, calmed the turmoil inside her.

'Are you wanting to get rid of me?' she asked at last, aware how stupid the words sounded even as she spoke them.

'You wouldn't believe me even if I pretended that I was,' James told her gently. 'It seems that Nicholas is without a secretary again. I can't continue to hog the best one we've ever had when he needs her so badly. But there's no dishonour, my dear, if you want to turn the suggestion down. Angela's only the most recent in a long line of girls who seem to have been defeated by him.'

'Perhaps he'd defeat me too,' Jenny suggested.

'I don't think so. Your fragile looks are very deceptive. Even Nicholas, who doesn't know you very well, is aware of a core of strength in you. But the main thing, of course, is that you won't irritate him by being stupid.'

'Is it what *you* want me to do?,' she asked slowly.

'I'd like you to help him,' James replied. 'Think about it and let me know.'

She nodded and walked back to her own room, thinking she knew what it felt like to sign her own death warrant. How long before she followed Angela and all the others out of the front door? Perhaps Fate was taking a hand, making sure that she didn't get too entrenched at Redfern's after all. The thought produced a grin that drove the look of doom from her face.

'That's better!' Gwen said bracingly. 'You looked ready to swallow a bottle of aspirins when you came in.'

'I was weighing up my chances of survival,' said Jenny with dignity.

'Of course you'll survive ... but I'm less sure Nicholas will!'

Jenny considered this cryptic utterance, decided she didn't know what to make of it, and went back to her own work. She saw nothing of Nicholas until the end of the day. She was tidying the desk in James's room ready for the next day when he suddenly walked in.

'Are you going to take me on?' The question was abrupt, but she wasn't looking at him to see that his eyes examined her face with some care.

'I'm going to try ... but the failure rate is rather high!'

'Partly my fault, but not entirely. You must tell me if I get too unreasonable, and I shall tell you if you do something I find irritating. Does that sound fair?'

She nodded, thinking that it sounded a joyless prospect and she'd been a fool not to stay with James. Nicholas fiddled with his father's paper-knife for a moment.

'You'll have a breathing space for a few days while Gwen finds a new girl for James. I'm going north till the weekend. Ainslie is trying to persuade me to go into politics. The sitting Member is going to retire because of ill-health. I must decide within the next couple of months whether I want to be a candidate.'

'I know law and politics often go together ... but would you enjoy a politician's life?' she asked curiously.

'Probably not, though both professions are thought to require the same streak of exhibitionism! I must be on my way ... thank you for putting your head into the lion's mouth, Jenny wren.' It just about summed it up, she decided grimly.

A pleasant, middle-aged woman called Helen Addison was hired to look after James, and there was time to show her the Redfern ropes before Nicholas came back. After that, life was never to be the same again. Jenny had imagined that she'd always worked hard, but she hadn't known what it was to be totally taken over ... every bit of energy and concentration that she possessed used by a man who drove himself even harder. It was rather like riding a whirlwind—dangerous but exciting. At the end of a fortnight nothing disastrous had happened, but she was uncomfortably aware that her own life had sunk without trace in Nicholas Redfern's. She never knew when she'd still be working at seven p.m. or rushing across London in a taxi with some paper he suddenly needed. She became familiar with the Law Courts, and sat, fascinated, through a hearing because he thought her impression of how it was going might be useful. There he was a stranger, disguised by the strange rituals of the law, until his voice and smile reminded her that this was the man who now monopolised her life. Watching him charm a nervous witness, or bludgeon an awkward one, it didn't take much imagination to see him in action on the floor of the House of Commons.

He didn't refer again to the subject of a political career and she began to think that he'd abandoned the idea of it. She was getting ready to go home one evening when, indirectly, the matter cropped up again.

'What are you going to do this weekend?' he demanded suddenly.

'What I usually do ... domestic chores and shopping, walk home via the Portobello Road for the fun of watching people haggle with the street traders. The boring young man in the flat below mine will try to invite himself to supper. I shall resist his advances and eat alone.'

'Doesn't sound all that exciting,' Nicholas commented. 'Why not come to the Midlands with me instead?'

As invitations went, it was vague—deliberately so, she thought.

'Tell me more,' she suggested calmly.

'I and Oliver and Freda—remember them?—are spending the weekend with the Ainslies at Greenhills. Mary asked if I could bring you too. I don't know whether you'd enjoy it, but it can hardly fail to be more interesting than the weekend you've got planned.'

He sounded so confident that she was strongly tempted to refuse, just for the pleasure of taking the wind out of his sails. But something in Lady Ainslie's request had sounded like a plea for help.

'I'll come,' she decided eventually. 'There's an awful fascination in the thought of seeing Arthur Ainslie on his home ground.'

Nicholas's mouth twitched into a smile but he shook his head warningly as well. 'Don't underestimate him; he's going to be a power in the land before he's through.'

The way that was said made Jenny look at him doubtfully, struck by an idea that seemed to explain something she'd found puzzling. 'Is that what attracts *you*? Do you want to be a "power" too?'

Nicholas didn't answer the question, only evaded it. 'You sound disapproving! Are you about to remind me that "power corrupts and absolute power corrupts absolutely?" '

He was still smiling, but a hint of steeliness in the dark eyes fastened on her suggested that he was also irritated. She supposed that she *had* sounded disapproving.

'I'm not going to remind you of anything except the fact that you're due in Lincoln's Inn in ten minutes' time.'

'Miss Bartlett disengages, I see . . . to retire from the battle, or merely to regroup her forces?'

'Miss Bartlett declines to say,' she answered prudently.

After a long stare he changed the subject. 'We're due in Warwickshire at tea-time on Saturday. I'll pick you up at eleven o'clock and we'll lunch on the way.'

No question, obviously, of whether this was the arrangement that would suit her. Hers not to reason why; hers to obey or die!

When Saturday morning came she changed her clothes three times, then, disgusted with such mindless dithering, finished up in the oatmeal tweed skirt and corduroy jacket she'd begun with. A checked wool shirt and rust-coloured sweater completed the outfit, and the only clothes she packed were a favourite scoop-necked cream cashmere sweater and long skirt checked in cream and brown to change into. Heaven knew what Freda Wheatley or the gorgeous Joanne would appear in for a country dinner party, but if the choice was to be under or over-dressed, Jenny knew which she preferred.

She had coffee beans ground and percolating by the time Nicholas arrived, in case he should like some before they set off. When she brought it in to him he was doing what she'd once done to him—examining her bookshelves and the rest of the private place she'd

made for herself. The room looked larger than it was
because it was arranged with the simplicity and
extreme neatness that he now associated with her. A
prie-dieu in one corner caught his eye; its green velvet
was rubbed with much use, but it was still beautiful.

'Nice,' he said appreciatively.

'It belonged to my grandfather and it's the most
precious thing I own.'

Cup in hand, he wandered over to a small table on
which two silver-framed photographs stood side by
side. One was of an elderly woman with decisive
features and an air of calm common sense. In the other
an old man stared at him with eyes full of integrity and
goodness—Canon Bartlett for a certainty. There was
no photograph of the man she'd expected to marry.
Nicholas wondered if she kept that for the privacy of
her bedroom, and was startled to discover how much
he disliked the idea.

His car was parked outside the house. She was
handed in a few minutes later, and the dark green
Jaguar slid noiselessly away from the kerb. Enclosed
in the intimacy of the car, she felt suddenly much too
aware of him—long brown hands resting on the wheel,
faint fresh smell of the after-shave lotion he'd used,
and altogether the sense that an overwhelmingly male
man was sitting a few inches away from her. If she
wasn't to fall apart she must take the initiative straight
away.

'*Very* luxurious,' she murmured, glancing around
the car. 'It's a far cry from the clapped-out old heap
Gramps used to coax around Cambridge. One honest-
to-goodness hill would have been too much for it.'

'You don't despise a little luxury, I hope,' said
Nicholas, edging them through the heavy traffic
funnelling on to the M4 going westward.

'I don't despise it . . . just don't feel at home with it.'

'She was poor but she was honest,' murmured a bland voice in her ear.

'Something like that!' It was hard to keep him at a distance when he made her laugh so easily.

'Well, your puritan conscience is in for a rough ride . . . Greenhills is pretty luxurious too.'

'I shall do my best to look as if I'm used to it.'

'Don't try too hard to look like anything you're not. We quite like you the way you are!'

He completed her confusion by removing one hand from the steering wheel and covering her own where it lay in her lap. What good was pertness when panic set in? What had possessed her to agree to come with him? She already saw too much of him for her own peace of mind. Nicholas registered her silence and took his eyes from the road for two seconds to look at her. Miss Bartlett was staring raptly out of the window at the delightful environs of Heathrow Airport. He relented to the extent of removing his hand, and began to talk matter-of-factly about the work Oliver Wheatley had already started on in Italy. After a little while her stampeding heart quietened again and she was able to take part in the conversation.

They left the motorway to turn northward, lunched at a village pub outside Oxford, and then drove at a leisurely pace through Woodstock and Stratford. It was half-past four when he swung the car into a driveway and stopped outside a large red-brick house set in grounds that Jenny described to herself as 'stately-municipal'—there was a great deal of shaven grass, manicured shrubs, and flower beds whose regiments of daffodils and tulips had surely been planted by an unimaginative gardener with a tape-measure. Still, the flowers themselves were beautiful, and beyond the formal gardens meadows flowed up to meet tree-covered hills. There was even an elegant horse or two dotted around the paddocks ... Sir Arthur, she realised, left no detail neglected.

They found the Wheatleys there before them, looking glad to see two new arrivals, and Mary Ainslie was relieved enough to go to the length of kissing Jenny's cheek.

'Glad you could come,' she murmured shyly.

'Your garden's beautiful,' said Jenny, struggling with herself. 'I've never seen such gorgeous spring flowers.'

'Yes ... but Baines *will* plant them in rows! I read somewhere that you're supposed to throw them down in handfuls. When I told him he snorted and went on doing it his way.'

'Tell him he's fired unless he does it *your* way next time,' Jenny smilingly suggested. 'There's no need to be intimidated unless he knows *more* than you do!'

Mary blinked at this revolutionary idea. 'I think you might be right,' she agreed slowly.

Nicholas had been right about the luxury of Greenhills—it was more sumptuously carpeted, more silkenly curtained than any house she'd ever seen. None of it was in poor taste, but Jenny found herself longing for just one shabby object. The bedroom allotted to her was a poem in peach and grey, and the bathroom had only to be shared with Joanne. Mary explained that her daughter was out at a point-to-point. She'd be back in time for dinner, bringing the young man she currently allowed to be useful to her, and the only other dinner guests would be the couple who had recently become their nearest neighbours.

'He's a stockbroker,' Lady Ainslie explained un-enthusiastically, 'and his wife's mad about horses.'

'So is Mrs Wheatley . . . I gather she spends a lot of time riding round Richmond Park.'

'You'd never think it,' Mary said vaguely. 'Still, it's a great help! Dear Nicholas will help with the stockbroker, so perhaps it won't be too bad. Arthur reckons that all you need for a successful party is a comfortable room and a lot of good food and drink . . . but I'm afraid there's more to it than that.'

Her anxious face prompted Jenny to lean forward suddenly and kiss her cheek. 'You worry too much. It's the duty of your guests to enjoy themselves, and it won't be your fault if they don't.'

Mary Ainslie hovered on the edge of a confession, then changed her mind to say instead, 'Nicholas says you're the most deceptively gentle little lamb who ever nibbled away at his ego . . . it was such a funny remark that I remembered it. If I understand his meaning, which I probably don't, I'm sure he wasn't right. You're the kindest woman I've ever met.'

She went away after that, leaving her guest to bathe and change before Joanne returned to take over the bathroom. Jenny lay in the scented water, pondering the remark that Mary had repeated. She didn't have any difficulty understanding it, and it made her feel remarkably cheerful. The thought that Nicholas might occasionally find her as destructive of his peace of mind as she found him sent her down to the drawing room presently with the joyous gaiety that transformed her into beauty. It also armoured her against an uncongenial host and a fellow-guest, the stockbroker, who took an ill-timed fancy to her. She allowed something for a man who was bored with a horse-mad wife, but it didn't make her sorry enough for him to have her knee stroked beneath the dining table. She turned her attention to Oliver Wheatley on her left hand and found him unexpectedly easy to talk to. The smooth, polished façade hid a more interesting man than she'd supposed, which perhaps accounted for the fact that Nicholas had made a friend of him.

Back in the drawing-room after a long and complicated dinner, Oliver strolled over to the piano and sat down to play the sort of music that no one else need listen to if they didn't feel inclined. Jenny looked round the room, thinking that the most skilful hostess on earth couldn't have welded this group of people into one party—Arthur Ainslie was telling his new neighbour what was wrong with the stock market; the neighbour's wife was going round the Badminton trial course fence by fence with Freda Wheatley; Joanne was displayed to great advantage on the rug at Nicholas's feet; and Mary Ainslie was doing her best to distract a young man's attention from the fact. In short, Jenny decided, there was no reason why she shouldn't please herself. She wandered over to the piano to listen to the café music that Oliver was playing so beautifully. It was the nicest discovery of the weekend so far that this talented man also had the lightest of touches in conducting a flirtation that was enjoyable but didn't have to be taken seriously. She wasn't aware of the moment when Nicholas managed to change places with the young man talking to Mary, but she did notice that he looked disapproving when they all eventually said good night.

'If I can tear you from Oliver's side in the morning, Jenny wren, we'll take a bracing walk together,' he murmured as they walked upstairs. 'He's normally a reserved man, but you seemed to be making a lot of progress with him.'

'Not nearly as much as you were making, though,' she said sweetly. 'It seemed to be touch and go whether Joanne actually seduced you on the hearth rug.'

'Jealous, by any chance?'

'Not in the least . . . good night, Nicholas.'

She sounded as if she meant it, damn her. He walked into his own room and shut the door unnecessarily hard.

Jenny rose in time for the eight o'clock service next morning and followed the directions Mary had given her the night before. It was a beautiful morning of early spring, with the colours of sky and earth looking as if they'd just been freshly enamelled. She found it a relief to be out of the opulently warm house, away from people putting pressures on each other. The church was small and simple, and the forthright priest who took the service would have been approved of by her grandfather. When she walked out of the dimness of the church into the brilliant sunshine it took her a moment to focus on the tall figure of Nicholas Redfern propped against a gravestone outside.

'Remember me . . . we had an assignation this morning?'

At any other time she might have resented the snide tone, but the morning was too beautiful, and she felt at peace with the world.

'You sound as though you're in need of breakfast,' Jenny said, smiling at him.

'Quite right . . . do you mind looking at our sleeping ancestors while we eat? If so, we'll find somewhere less sheltered but more lively.'

Jenny stared at him. 'You mean a . . . a picnic?'

Nicholas picked up the holdall at his feet. 'Here we have the works, kindly provided by Mary . . . orange juice, ham rolls and a thermos of coffee. I couldn't face the thought of Oliver ogling you over the breakfast table.'

'I think I'd rather do without breakfast if you're going to go on being disagreeable,' she said quietly.

After a moment's silence in which she expected to see him walk away, taking breakfast with him, he gave her the charming smile that now and then chased all cynicism from his face.

'Rebuke merited, Jenny wren. I'll apologise for being surly and we'll start again. Now, where would my lady like to sit?'

With the absurdly self-important air of a bad head-waiter he led her to a sheltered horizontal slab in one corner of the churchyard, dusted its mossy top, and laid out the silk handkerchief from his breast pocket as a table cloth. She remembered the al fresco meal that followed for the rest of her life . . . no ham rolls would ever be as succulent again, no coffee as fragrant. No company, alas, would be as good. She fed the last of the rolls to a ring of expectant sparrows who had materialised out of nowhere, and dusted down her skirt.

'It's been lovely, Nicholas, but I can't help feeling we ought to go back to our hosts. Mary and Freda find each other heavy going.'

He nodded and began to repack the holdall with an abstracted air, then stopped to look at her.

'I told Arthur last night that I'd made up my mind, Jenny. He's going to put my name forward as a Parliamentary candidate. I have the feeling that you don't altogether approve of the idea.'

'It hardly matters whether I do or not.'

'Don't beg the question . . . I'm asking you.'

She looked away from eyes that seemed to be examining all her shameful little fears and withdrawals. 'I suppose my views are coloured by the ones I grew up with. Gramps had no time for churchmen who meddled in what he thought of as political issues, but he didn't have much time for politicians either. Cynical or self-interested, he judged most of them to be.'

'Which label applies to me?'

'I don't know . . . perhaps neither,' she answered uncertainly.

'And perhaps the citizens of this constituency won't elect me . . . so we may never know.'

'Not elect you? Don't be silly. They'll do what Sir Arthur tells them!'

'I'd forgotten him for the moment. Yes, you're probably right.'

His hands suddenly clamped themselves on her shoulders and swung her round to face him. 'You won't desert me, Jenny wren, even though you disapprove of politics?' He asked the question so gravely that she knew she was meant to take it seriously. That moment, too, she would remember, because a blackbird began to fill the silence with his liquid song.

'I won't desert you,' she promised at last.

He leaned forward and gently kissed her mouth. 'Now I suppose we really must go back though what I'd rather do is walk you over the hills and far away.'

CHAPTER FIVE

WHEN breakfast was finished Nicholas's light-hearted mood dropped away again and they walked back to Greenhills almost in silence. The house was in sight when he said suddenly, 'You're a very restful woman to be with, Jenny.'

'A charming way of saying dull?' she queried with a smile.

'Not at all . . . and you damned well know it! We've spent enough time together by now for you to be aware that I say what I mean.'

'Then I'm sorry I looked a genuine compliment in the mouth!'

He took hold of her hand casually—just in case Oliver should be watching, she supposed. It was a dog-in-the-manger attitude that surprised her in a man who had very few ungenerous instincts.

Mary Ainslie looked relieved to see them back and immediately carried Jenny off to inspect her kitchen garden. Nicholas was pounced on by his host, but by the time the garden party returned Joanne had inveigled him into playing her at billiards. Skin-tight black trousers and a white sweater hugging every curve were presumably intended to keep her opponent's attention anywhere but on the game. Miss Ainslie wasn't subtle, but she had her father's irresistible vitality and his contempt for old-fashioned considerations; me and mine, and thee and thine wouldn't come into her scheme of things. She saw no reason not to take what she wanted, and it looked very much as if she wanted Nicholas Redfern.

When they left for London after tea she and her father also came out dressed for travelling. Suspicion that Nicholas was giving them a lift back to London became a certainty when Joanne promptly settled herself in the seat beside the driver. Jenny felt depression settle on her like a dead weight, and blamed it unfairly on Mary's delicious but very large lunch. She'd have liked to know whether Nicholas regretted the travelling arrangements, but his face gave nothing away as usual. Jenny thought he was probably amused by Joanne's tactics. He wasn't a man to bother with vain pursuit; if surrender wasn't immediately forthcoming, he would simply go on to a more likely prospect. In the case of Miss Ainslie, he'd got someone prepared to meet him more than half-way ... even less trouble than usual!

Jenny did her best to look pleasant as Sir Arthur settled himself beside her. It made the next two hours a penance, but he'd just been a generous host and she must do her best to talk to him civilly. She must also remember that Nicholas's future seemed to be bound up with him. Her very thought seemed to put words into his mouth.

'Nicholas told you about his new career, Miss Bartlett?'

She slewed round in her seat to find his eyes fixed on her, bright as pebbles and just as penetrating.

'Yes, he told me—but the career's not quite certain, surely? He's got to be adopted as a candidate first, quite apart from fighting an election.'

'Your heart not in it? Doesn't sound like it to me.'

In the front seat Joanne was doing her best to keep the driver's mind off the road; all the same, Jenny wondered how much of the conversation in the back of the car he was managing to listen to. She was familiar by now with the number of different things his mind could grapple with at once.

'It hardly matters whether *my* heart's in it or not,' she murmured. Ainslie gave an irritated snort and she was suddenly prompted to be honest with him. 'If you really want to know, I'm not hell-bent on seeing Nicholas in Parliament.'

'Why not?' The question was rapped at her like a bullet from a gun. 'Don't think it matters what happens to this country, I suppose . . . it's something for other people to worry about.'

Jenny was nettled by the catechism, and tired of having words put into her mouth.

'I think it matters very much indeed, but the less politicians are allowed to meddle, the better the country seems to do, on the whole.'

It was rash, and the sort of sweeping statement Nicholas would have made her justify if he'd heard it.

'War with a vengeance, Arthur,' he suddenly murmured from the front seat.

Ainslie's lips moved in what Jenny realised was meant to be a grin. 'There's something in what you say, Miss Bartlett,' he admitted surprisingly, 'but it proves *my* point completely! What you say wouldn't be true if we had men like Nicholas in Parliament— tough, clever, and honest. So put your back into it and shove like the rest of us.'

Feeling that she'd been chided, Jenny glanced up and met Nicholas's eyes in the driving mirror, full of amused understanding. But the subject was allowed to rest there; Sir Arthur wanted to study the papers in his lap, and she could give up the effort of talking to him. The car stopped outside her front door just long enough for her to thank them for the visit, then purred on its way again, presumably taking them to dine together.

Jenny walked into a flat that seemed cramped and airless after the spaciousness of Greenhills. Rich living was unsettling, and she told herself she'd do better to stay where she was in future. The truth of what really ailed her was harder to face, but in the course of a long evening she finally managed it. Nicholas Redfern wasn't a man to feel lukewarm about. If you couldn't hate him—and she doubted if the woman was born who could do that—you found that he'd walked into your life and taken it over. It was something to be necessary to him during the working day, but it wasn't enough. She couldn't go on being picked up and given a ride in his life occasionally because there wasn't another companion handy; still less because he sometimes remembered that she might be lonely. She was a useful extension of his own right hand, but he would never see her as anything else, and the bleak decision to be taken was simply how much longer she could bear to stay. From Nicholas's point of view, she ought to go before his life got even more complicated, even though James would be bitterly disappointed, and Ainslie would regard it as desertion before a battle she had no stomach for.

When she went into the office next morning there was no sign of Nicholas. She was thinking sourly that a late night with Joanne had disturbed his usual routine when he appeared looking as if he hadn't been to bed at all. He was grey with tiredness, and the sweater and slacks he wore confirmed that things were not as normal.

'Upheaval last night,' he explained briefly. 'James had a heart attack . . . fortunately after I got back.'

'Oh, Nicholas . . . I'm so sorry! Where is he?'

'Still in the Brompton at the moment. He's much better this morning, but they're keeping him there for rest and observation.'

Jenny looked at his drawn face, thinking that his affections weren't usually so visible for the world to see. 'I hope you're not thinking of doing your father's work as well as your own today. You look worn out.'

'I must sort out one or two urgent things with Andrew; then I might sneak upstairs for an hour or two.'

'James *is* going to be all right . . .?' she asked quietly.

'He assures me he is! The future's got to be thought about, though. In fact, I seem to have spent a very long night sitting by his bed, doing just that.' The expression on her face made him smile at her with sudden sweetness. 'Don't worry about him, Jenny wren. He's a tough old bird, thank God!'

She saw no more of Nicholas for the rest of the morning, but soon after lunch his buzzer sent her hurrying along the hall, notebook in hand. He was staring at some papers in front of him when she went in, but his dark gaze flicked over her—flyaway fringe of brown hair falling over her forehead as usual, severely neat office clothes: forest green sweater and plaid skirt, and shirt collar crisply white against the creamy skin of her throat. She sat down always with a minimum of fuss, and none of the self-advertising tricks he was accustomed to in secretaries wanting to attract his attention. He looked at her quiet face, and was suddenly stabbed by a feeling of apprehension. His own life was in a state of turmoil at the moment, but it didn't give him the right to involve her in it too. She'd had to battle hard enough for the peace of mind she seemed to have recovered. He hesitated on the very edge of deciding that he must change his mind. Then she looked up, wondering what they were waiting for, and he knew he couldn't change his mind.

'Put that damned pencil down; I want to talk to you.'

His harsh voice frightened her with the sudden fear that James had got worse during the day, but before she could frame a question Nicholas was speaking again.

'There's a lot to say, but I don't know where to begin ... with last night's goings-on, I suppose. Sitting by James's bed, I started to think about the changes we must make here. By the mercy of God I wasn't away last night, but I might easily have been. In future there must always be someone around. A housekeeper living on top of him in his own quarters would fret him more than she would help, and the obvious answer is for me to move out so that she can take over the top floor—be independent, in fact, but immediately within reach.'

Nicholas drove a hand through his dark hair, making it more untidy than ever. 'Odd how life puts threads in your hand that insist on weaving themselves into a pattern. The need to house a companion for James fits very neatly into a need of my own. Now that I've agreed to offer myself as a candidate in Ainslie's constituency I've also had to accept the fact that at the moment I'm a mixed blessing to the cause —a man with a much-publicised divorce behind him, thanks to my ex-wife, and something of a reputation! God knows why, except that gossip-writers like to stick labels on people. I need to be made respectable, apparently; in other words, to become a married man again.'

Jenny felt her heart stumble, then reluctantly plod

on with its job. She supposed it was good of Nicholas to explain all these personal details to her, but it was very little to do with her that he was going to make Joanne Ainslie his second wife. Every nerve in her own body might protest that the choice was suicidal, but from anybody else's point of view he would be thought to have done very well for himself. She made a heroic effort to pin an expression of polite interest on her face and waited for what seemed like an eternity.

'I wondered if *you'd* consider marrying me, my dear Jenny wren.'

His voice was deliberate as usual, and the very ordinariness of it heightened her impression that some monstrous joke was being played on her.

'You're . . . you can't be serious,' she stuttered at last. 'We agreed not long ago that we'd both been put off matrimony.'

'That's what prompts my suggestion. My personal preference has to give way to the fact that I must find a wife, but a nominal marriage isn't much to offer a woman. Then I remembered the one girl it might just appeal to . . . a girl who was no more anxious than I am to get entangled in emotion again. Even better, this same girl has a longing for domesticity. We already know that we manage the difficult business of working together rather well; it doesn't seem impossible that we could live together happily. Does it still sound preposterous?'

'I don't know *how* it sounds,' she confessed unevenly. The faint colour in her cheeks had faded, leaving her very pale, but she managed to look squarely at him.

'I'll have to think about it. It *is* a marriage in name only you're talking about?'

'Yes . . . unless we both decided eventually that it

could be turned into something else.'

'Only one of us might want to,' she pointed out.

'Yes,' he said again, 'but that's a risk we'd have to agree to take.'

'The whole idea's full of risks.' She despised herself for sounding nervous, but she could have sworn that the smile suddenly transforming his face was full of joyous confidence.

'Life's full of danger, Jenny. That's what makes it so interesting!'

'Yes . . . well, I'll have to think about it,' she said again.

She released her desperate grip on the shorthand pad in her lap and got stiffly to her feet. He was at the door before her, and stood looking down at her for a moment without opening it.

'No dishonour, my dear, if you turn the idea down. We simply go on here as before.'

They were the words James had used to her once before, and the recollection swung her mind back to a man who would be overjoyed to have her as a daughter-in-law. She nodded to Nicholas, and walked back to her own room. By Heaven's grace Gwen was still closeted with Andrew, and too busy when she finally emerged to notice that her room-mate for the rest of the afternoon was untalkative to the point of unaccustomed rudeness.

The weekend that followed was the most unsettling she'd ever spent in her life. One moment time dragged unbearably, the next, the clock was ticking at ten times its normal rate. Jenny didn't know whether to be more terrified that Monday would arrive with her no nearer making up her mind, or that it would never come at all and she'd spend the rest of her life in her present state of dither. Her flat, draughty in winter and too hot in summer, suddenly became too precious to leave, until the joy of planting a garden and watching it blossom crept insidiously into her mind. She'd made herself into a highly competent secretary but office life didn't satisfy her in the way that it did Gwen Marriot; she could leave it without a qualm. Her fevered mind did its best to grapple logically with the problem. In one side of the scales she heaped all the good she could see in Nicholas's suggestion—a solution to his anxiety about James, the 'respectable' façade he needed for himself, and for her the satisfaction of creating an attractive, comfortable home. About that, at least, she didn't have any doubt. The home she made would be attractive, and well-run, and even the most unpromising chunk of ground could be turned into a garden.

Looked at like that, the left-hand side of the scale looked quite full. Then she put into the other side the simple overriding fact that her beautiful new home and garden would have to be shared with a man she'd already decided she must part company with. If she couldn't bear to stay and work for him, living in the same house would be an impossibility.

Monday finally came, and she went back to Hans Place almost convinced that she'd made up her mind. There was a note on her desk and she felt weak with relief at the sight of it. Nicholas had changed his mind . . . thought better of the whole preposterous idea. But the note merely explained that a weekend telephone call had sent him unexpectedly to Birmingham for the day. It was a temporary reprieve, and she could force her mind to think about other things. Gwen shot a glance at her strained face, and muttered a laconic 'Feeling all right?' in her direction, but otherwise left her in peace. At lunchtime Nicholas rang.

'Jenny, I hoped to get back this afternoon, but there's still a lot to do here. I've a favour to ask, of course. Could you go and see James for me this evening? It's a long day for him without a visitor.'

Her heart resumed its normal beat, and her voice was warm with the relief of knowing that here was something she could do for him without question.

'Of course . . . I'd love to go. Shall I tell him you'll be there tomorrow?'

'Yes, please . . . I'm very grateful. Give him my love.'

He rang off, disinclined, as always, to waste words, but she sat thinking afterwards that, whether she wanted it to happen or not, she was being drawn into the life of the Redfern family. James was out of bed when she got to the hospital that evening—still in pyjamas and dressing gown, but having progressed to the point of being allowed to sit in an armchair.

'There's nothing wrong with Nicholas,' she said quickly, interpreting the anxiety in his face. 'He had to make an unexpected dash up to Birmingham. I'm deputising, but he'll be back to see you tomorrow.'

'Jenny, my dear . . . *you'll* do my stock much more good! My friends here are going to be very jealous!'

She smiled in the direction of the three other patients in the small side ward—all indeed staring at her with great interest—then turned back to James. He looked unfamiliar—shrunken and suddenly rather old.

'You must be better or you wouldn't be out of bed,' she said cheerfully, then touched his hand by way of apology. 'Sorry . . . did that sound unbearably rallying? It's the dreadful effect hospitals have on visitors!'

'You sounded kind, as always,' James insisted. 'I *am* better, and I can't wait to go home.'

His hand trembled under her own, making her even more sharply aware of the change in him. Sudden illness had left him frightened and unsure of everything he'd previously taken for granted. She thought of her own state when she'd first gone to Redfern's— James had never pried into what had made her unhappy, but she'd been comforted by so many small acts of kindness from him. She loved him, and hated to see him so diminished now.

'It's a funny thing, Jenny,' James said quietly. 'You go marching along, imagining that you're going to live for ever, then suddenly the truth catches up with you. That's when you miss a woman in your life. Nicholas, marvellous though he is, doesn't have quite the same touch!'

He smiled in case she should find what he'd just said sad, and briskly turned the conversation to office affairs. She answered him coherently—or supposed that she did, because he didn't complain that she wasn't making sense. Inwardly she was only concerned with the fact that her problem had just been settled. One wistful sentence from James had been enough to end the confusion raging in her mind. She was going to marry Nicholas Redfern. The knowledge of how much pleasure it would give James was in the smile she offered him. He was beginning to look tired, though, and she kissed him good night and went away before she was tempted to say what must be left to Nicholas to tell him.

CHAPTER SIX

THERE were more important problems to think about but Jenny spent most of the night trying to decide how to respond to a business offer of marriage. By letter? 'Dear Nicholas, on reflection I think it would be a Good Idea to marry you.' Perhaps interrupt a session of dictation one morning, or add it to the string of messages always waiting for him on his desk? Each idea seemed worse than the last. Having brought herself to the pitch of deciding to marry him, she thought the whole scheme might founder because she could find no way of telling him so.

She was sorting papers the following morning and having to do half of them again because her mind wasn't on the job when Nicholas walked in.

'I spoke to Father a moment ago . . . he swore your visit last night made a new man of him. Thank you for going.'

'Pleasure,' she said mechanically. It might have helped James, but it seemed to have destroyed her. She went on sorting as though her life depended on it, unaware—because she refused to look at him—that he was amusedly watching the mess she was making of it.

'K comes before L,' he felt obliged to point out at last.

'I never can remember,' said Jenny crossly. She looked up, saw the laughter in his eyes, and suddenly it seemed possible after all to say what she had to say.

'If you still want to go ahead with it, I've decided that the . . . the arrangement you mentioned would be all right with me.'

There was such a total silence in the room that she was afraid he'd forgotten what the arrangement was and was now desperately trying to remember. If he did remember, had he expected her to turn it down, or hoped she would because he'd since had an idea he liked better? She went hot and cold by turns, waiting for him to say anything at all. He was unaware of the delay, taken up with the discovery that relief could do strange things to a man. The inmates of Redfern's would think he'd gone mad if he suddenly started turning handsprings in front of them, but something like that would work off the current of elation leaping inside him. Jenny hadn't sounded exactly enthusiastic, but, praise Heaven, she'd had the great good sense to see how ideal was the 'arrangement'. He might have known she'd have no truck with dramatising herself and the situation between them. As women went, she was almost without wiles, and he was thankful for the fact; he'd had enough of them to last a lifetime.

'I'm very glad, Jenny wren,' he said at last, when she'd almost given up hope of hearing him speak again. No flowery speeches, but had she really expected them? Even if he wasn't the least fulsome of men, she must keep strongly in mind the nominal nature of their marriage. The situation called for simple directness, and that's what she'd get from him.

'There's a lot to talk about,' Nicholas said next. 'Can we have dinner together this evening, when I get back from the hospital?'

'I could be cooking it while you're there?' she suggested. 'It's an occupation I find calming!'

'Poor girl . . . is that what you feel in need of?'

She nodded, aware that her voice suddenly wasn't to be trusted. He walked over to her, and took her own ice-cold hands in his warm ones. 'Don't look so anxious ... it's going to work out beautifully.' Her hand was suddenly lifted to his mouth and kissed, and the gesture, so unexpectedly graceful and tender, was almost the undoing of her.

'See you this evening,' he said, and walked out of the room.

It suited her very well that she was left to work on her own for the rest of the day. She made a lunchtime raid on Harrods' Food Hall in case the refrigerator upstairs was stocked with only its usual iron rations, but although her laden basket was noted by Gwen's eagle eye, nothing was said until Nicholas looked in to confirm that he'd be back from the hospital about seven-thirty.

'What gives ... tell Aunt Gwen,' she wanted to know as soon as she heard the front door slam.

Jenny gave a little shrug that was meant to suggest an evening ahead devoid of the smallest excitement, but Miss Marriot still watched her like a terrier at a rabbit-hole.

'Nicholas has gone to visit James,' Jenny said casually.

'That I think I can just manage to guess! It's the rest I want to know about. Why should Nicholas bother to tell you what time he's getting back? You won't still be here working, I hope.'

'I said I'd cook supper for him ... nothing to get worked up about,' Jenny confessed, driven into a corner.

'Did you indeed? I suppose you're going to tell me you feel sorry for the poor fellow.'

'I'm not going to tell you anything at all!'

Jenny's smile took the sting out of the words, but Gwen knew when she was beaten. Jenny Bartlett, so

gently amenable on the surface, had a rock-bottom
stubbornness that a mule wouldn't have disowned.
Gwen buttoned herself into her raincoat in silence, but
allowed herself a Parthian shot just as she was going
out of the door.

'Something's going on! Can't quite put my finger on
it yet, but I'm never wrong. I shall be bitterly offended
if I'm the last to be told what it is.'

She grinned forgiveness of her room-mate's cagi-
ness and banged her way out of the front door. Jenny
was relieved to see her go; she wasn't ready yet for
Gwen to make a wild leap and land on the
unbelievable truth; she must come to terms with it
herself first. She switched off the office lights and
climbed the stairs to a room that was now becoming
familiar to her.

By the time Nicholas reappeared, she was happily
lost in the dish she was preparing—the sautéed
chicken was keeping warm in the oven, rice and
courgettes were almost ready, and she was thickening
a sauce compounded of stock, garlic, orange and
lemon juice, and a generous dollop of his best dry
sherry. He walked into the kitchen, glasses of
vermouth in his hands, sniffing appreciatively.

'A little something to keep the cook going,' he said,
handing her a glass. 'The aroma tells me that some real
cooking is going on. We're not about to dine off some
reheated made-up 'serves two,' inextricably welded to
silver foil.'

'Certainly not . . . there's no fun in that. How was
James this evening?'

'Looking bored when I arrived, transformed by the
time I left. He could hardly believe it when I told him
you were prepared to throw in your lot with the
Redferns. He's overjoyed, Jenny.'

It was the wrong time to remember James's ambition to become a grandfather.

'You haven't changed your mind, I hope,' Nicholas observed quietly, seeing the sadness in her face.

'No . . . but I'm still not entirely used to the idea.'

The chicken was all that she'd hoped, and he ate the food with an enjoyment that pleased her. It wasn't until they were back in the sitting-room drinking the coffee which he rightly insisted he could make very well, that Nicholas switched the conversation back to themselves.

'I told James we'd be looking for a house to move into, not too far away, and casually aired the possibility that this flat might be used by a companion-housekeeper for him.'

'How did that idea go down?'

'Surprisingly well, because he remembered that a pleasant spinster cousin he knows and likes has just become homeless. A similar job with an elderly relative has just come to an end, for the reason you might expect. James thinks she'd be glad to be offered another one, and from Lorna Kennet's point of view he'll be a much easier proposition than the old battleaxe she's been living with for years.'

'Sounds ideal,' Jenny agreed, toying with her coffee cup. Nicholas watched her downbent face, wondering whether to creep up on the next fence or take it all standing.

'Now, about us,' he began gently. 'I've got a feeling that you're a country girl at heart, but will you settle for riverside London for the time being? I don't want to put too much ground between us and James, or do more travelling than I have to. Somewhere between here and the airport would be ideal, say Chiswick or Barnes.'

Jenny nodded, thinking that where they lived was the least of her worries.

The fence was right in front of him; nothing to do but fling himself at it. 'No point in hanging about. I've got to press on in the constituency, so the sooner we get the wedding out of the way the better . . . I'd suggest a special licence next week.' Her tiny gasp checked but didn't stop him. 'There's plenty of room for you here while we dispose of your flat and find a house.'

There was no mistaking the stark panic in her face. Nicholas waited to hear her say that she'd changed her mind about marrying him. She knew it was what she would have said if he'd made the smallest move towards her. Instead, he simply refilled her coffee cup, waiting for the outcome of the turmoil going on inside her. His hand wasn't entirely steady, but Jenny was in no state to notice the fact.

'I can't . . . can't say I . . . know Barnes from Chiswick,' she muttered at last, with tremendous difficulty.

He should have felt relieved, but the emotion suddenly overwhelming him was heart-stopping regret. The sound of his own voice confidently accepting that their peculiar marriage held a risk or two echoed in his ears. He didn't want a marriage of convenience with Jenny Bartlett . . . dear God, he *wanted* to marry her! But he was stuck with this farcical arrangement of his own proposing, and Jenny was so far from wanting to change the terms as to be close to backing out of it altogether. Almost, the words that they'd made a ridiculous mistake formed themselves in his mind. But if she saw it as another rejection . . . ? Nicholas replaced his cup on the table and smiled at her. 'Barnes or Chiswick . . . either way, we'll have a splendid view of the Boat Race!'

That evening marked the end of the peaceful, lonely life Jenny had carved for herself since leaving Cambridge. Afterwards, she was on a helter-skelter ride, being bumped from side to side and hurtling up and down at a speed that left her breathless. All she could find to be grateful for was the fact that this headlong progress left her no time to remember how frightened she was.

Nicholas wasted no time in announcing their engagement; a note was sent to *The Times*, and the Redfern staff told the very next morning. Jenny was conscious of Andrew's suddenly blank face, aware that the news had taken him by surprise and hurt him. She certainly hadn't given him much encouragement to fall in love with her, but instinct told her that at this moment it was what he was telling himself he'd done.

'Nothing to get excited about, indeed.' This was Gwen muttering in her ear, unfairly remembering her words and using them against her. 'The poor old antennae are failing,' Gwen added with a touch of sadness. 'Time was when I wouldn't have needed to be told about something like this happening under my very nose.'

Jenny longed to be able to tell her that superhuman powers of divination would have been required in this case, but it was out of the question. She'd agreed with Nicholas that their marriage was to appear normal to the rest of the world. Andrew roused himself to produce champagne from some secret source in his room, and the engagement was celebrated with the sort of banter that Jenny found it hard to know how to deal with. Nicholas was affable, but careful not to allow it to go on for too long. By the time everyone had settled down to work again, she hoped the worst was over, apart from the wedding ceremony itself.

Back in their own office again, Gwen bemoaned the need to start looking for a new secretary for Nicholas. 'I adore him, as you know, and I'm quite attached to you ... but I wish to Heaven you'd decided to marry anyone but each other. I've quite enjoyed life recently. Now the dreary procession will start again—nice incompetent women Nicholas fires, and competent bitches who walk out after a week or two.'

'Sorry,' Jenny murmured penitently. 'It's a bore for you, poor Gwen.'

There was something the Marriot antennae—clearly past all hope—were still failing to pick up. Nicholas was the most self-controlled of men, and Jenny Bartlett didn't make a habit of laying out her feelings for all to see, but the pair of them were surely the most restrained lovers that had ever *not* embarrassed the rest of the world with outward signs of affection. Gwen worded a question carefully in her mind before asking it.

'Shall you like being what the Americans call a 'domestic executive?' No regrets about giving up your independence?'

She got a blinding smile in return that almost reassured her.

'None at all ... I'm not one of your dyed-in-the-wool career girls. I yearn to be domestic ... bake bread, grow herbs, order a house so that people can come into it and feel comforted. I think *that's* what I might be really competent at.'

Gwen was too fascinated by an outlook so different from her own to notice that there was no mention of a husband on Jenny's list.

'Extraordinary! Seems a wicked waste to me of the best secretary we've ever had apart from me, but if that sort of thing makes you happy, I suppose there's no more to be said.'

She relapsed into silence, but then thought of one more thing that needed to be said.

'I suppose you know you've taken Andrew by surprise? I thought he was the one who was going to carry you off on his beautiful white charger. The dark horse always seems to win in the end.'

'I think I was just useful in bringing Emily up to scratch,' Jenny muttered hopefully.

'Then I hope it never matters that you should be able to judge what a man thinks about you,' said Miss Marriot thoughtfully.

Jenny hoped so too, because she was even more doubtful about her performance than Gwen was. Her understanding with people was usually immediate and sure, but Luke Armitage had destroyed her confidence where a man she loved was concerned, and Nicholas's emotions were a mystery to her. But he was unexpectedly patient and helpful in the tedious business of getting her installed in her temporary new home. The flat in Bayswater was put in the hands of a local estate agent and was sold to the first prospective buyer who came to look at it. She included most of the contents in the sale, but transferred to Hans Place all her own books, china and glass, and one or two cherished items of furniture—like Gramps's prie-dieu, and her grandmother's little writing desk and Victorian sewing chair. These things were inserted without any difficulty into Nicholas's vast room and had the effect of making her feel less of a stranger there. All the same, it was an extraordinary feeling to close the door on her own flat for the last time, and accept that her only home was now with a man she'd barely exchanged a dozen words with two months before. Thought about like that, what she was doing seemed the height of madness, and her grandmother must surely be signalling from heaven that young Jenny was about to come a cropper again. But although she didn't know how it had come about, her life was now bound up with Nicholas Redfern. Where her heart stood in the matter was something she must learn to keep to herself.

Her final journey from the flat was made with luggage containing all her clothes. Nicholas struggled up the narrow stairs with them and led the way to a quiet bedroom overlooking the back of the house.

'Dolly got this ready for you,' he said casually. 'There is another one to choose from, but it's rather cramped. The bathroom—unlike our bedrooms—we shall have to share!'

'This is . . . is fine,' Jenny said quickly, grateful to have the matter of the bedrooms made crystal clear, and careful not to look at him. Like James, Nicholas required a housekeeper, not a wife; he was only going to the trouble of getting one because a political career required a respectable set-up in the background.

James was allowed out of hospital at the end of the week and she went with Nicholas to fetch him home, glad to be doing something that a normal fiancée might naturally have done. He was so thankful to be home, and so content to think that Lorna Kennet was going to be happy as well, that Jenny's own wavering morale was stiffened.

'My dear . . . I'm so delighted that for two pins I'd burst into song,' said James, from the comfort of his own fireside chair. 'Just think of it . . . I needn't worry about Nicholas or you any more. And with dear Lorna upstairs, you don't need to worry about me. Peace of mind all round!'

Jenny wondered. Just now and then the suspicion occurred to her that Nicholas's mind wasn't as peaceful as James supposed. It wasn't surprising: even an odd sort of marriage like theirs would restrict him to some extent, however lightly the agreement was made to operate. One evening, when he was more abstracted than usual, it was on the tip of her tongue to ask why he hadn't done what the Ainslies must have expected. Joanne would have galloped to the altar with him, for sure. In the end she didn't ask the question because she thought she already knew the answer. He'd tried tying himself to a woman who made constant demands upon him. Joanne had had twenty years' practice in the art of getting her own way, and he probably thought it was too late to persuade her to change her habits now. She was an amusing, provocative companion, not the trouble-free and competent organiser of his home represented by Jenny Bartlett. Nicholas had arranged his life exactly as he wanted it. Having agreed to the arrangement, she must simply make the best of it, instead of whining to herself that it wasn't what she wanted after all!

CHAPTER SEVEN

THEY were married the following week on what the calendar insisted was the first official day of spring. Jenny awoke to the sound of rain—no Chaucerian 'shoure sweete', but a relentless downpour that flung itself against her window, mocking the possibility that this could be anybody's wedding day. By mid-morning it had begun to sound less confident, and at noon there was even a watery gleam or two of sun to rout the remaining drizzle.

To save James exertion, only Andrew and Gwen were to be their witnesses at the register office, but he, Lorna, Emily, and a handful of other friends had been invited to a lunch party at the Hyde Park Hotel, just along the road from Hans Place. When Jenny asked about the Ainslies, Nicholas had shaken his head.

'They'll still be in Italy . . . Arthur's inspecting the beginnings of his new village there.'

The list of names Nicholas had written down contained none supplied by Jenny, and he apologised for the fact.

'Sorry, my dear . . . what an oversight! Tell me who you'd like to invite.'

'No takers, thank you all the same.'

'You mean you don't have *any* friends or family, or just none that you care enough about to ask?'

'My family consists of a few remote cousins, who probably wouldn't trouble themselves to make a journey to London. The friends I had in Cambridge I deliberately left behind.'

'It doesn't sound like Jenny Bartlett to be so ruthless!'

He said it lightly, but she felt a hint of disapproval in him—as if it wasn't how friends were meant to be treated.

'As it happened, they were Luke's friends too,' she pointed out quietly. 'They'd have had to choose between him and me, and he was the one to go on living there.'

'No London friends?'

The colour rose under her clear skin. 'No . . . even though it does sound as if I'd been in hiding. Perhaps I have!'

He didn't press the point, being occupied with discovering in himself some very contrary emotions. It would have been a pleasure to strangle Luke Armitage for destroying her confidence so completely; on the other hand, if the man hadn't been the fool he undoubtedly was, Jenny would never have come to London. Against all the odds, Armitage's treachery hadn't made her bitter, but she was even more wary than he was himself of getting emotionally involved with people again. In rare moments of depression Nicholas doubted whether the damage to either of them was reparable. They were a couple of emotional cripples, and it was anybody's guess whether they would succeed in mending themselves in the course of mending each other.

Jenny dressed for her wedding, warmed by the memory of James Redfern shyly putting a package into her hand the night before. She'd found a ring inside, of emeralds set beautifully in antique gold. Apart from the loveliness of the thing itself, her pleasure lay in the fact that he should have wanted to give it to her at all. James explained that it had been his gift to his wife when Nicholas was born. Jenny realised that it had never been offered to his first daughter-in-law, and it made the gift all the more precious to her.

She was ready to leave when Nicholas tapped at her door, but stupidly reluctant to abandon the safety of her room.

'Almost time to go, Jenny . . . Andrew and Gwen are here.'

She opened the door but still stood hesitating, waiting for she knew not what—reassurance, perhaps, that they weren't about to do something they were both going to regret. Her cream wool suit reminded him of an eighteenth-century riding habit—its waist very nipped-in and its skirt very full—and the effect was heightened by a bowler of cream velour whose veiling, swathing the up-turned brim, just reached and dramatised her eyes. She looked so beautiful that Nicholas Redfern—articulate, unimpressionable, and difficult-to-please Mr Redfern—was completely at a loss for words.

'You've . . . done me very proud, Jenny wren,' he murmured inadequately.

She hadn't expected to throw Nicholas off balance and the knowledge that she had, even if it was only for a moment or two, did a great deal for her own peace of mind.

'You're looking very elegant yourself, if I'm allowed to say so!'

His smile told her that he'd recovered himself. 'Andrew's doing . . . he insisted that the occasion demanded a new suit. So, *me voilà*, as the French say!' Instead of walking with her into the sitting-room he was deflected into the hall by the sound of the telephone ringing. Jenny went into the room alone, to

be greeted by Gwen with a posy of flame-coloured
rosebuds.

'I thought you'd want our friend at the stall to be
represented,' she remarked drily. 'I'd have brought the
hound as well, but I couldn't tear him away from an
old shoe he was lunching off.'

Andrew was smiling at Gwen, but when he bent to
kiss Jenny his quiet 'Be happy, my dear' was meant for
her ears alone. She thought she must pin her hopes on
Emily or feel downright guilty about him.

When Nicholas came back into the room they were
laughing again, but he didn't miss the expression in
Andrew Fox's eyes. Someone else had been thrown by
the sight of Jenny in her wedding rig.

'That was Arthur Ainslie on the telephone,'
Nicholas said. 'They're home from Italy sooner than
expected—in fact I get the impression that they cut
their visit short deliberately.'

'So you asked them to join the lunch party,' Jenny
suggested calmly.

'Afraid so, my dear. I know you don't exactly warm
to Arthur, but it wouldn't occur to him that he wasn't
welcome.'

'Look on the bright side,' Andrew advised cheerfully. 'He's bound to stagger in with a couple of silver
salvers that you can flog for a small fortune
afterwards.'

'We've already had a very generous wedding
present,' Jenny said primly, then smiled in spite of
herself. 'It was a perfectly hideous oil painting, chosen
probably because I once rashly insisted that I
preferred water-colours!'

Nicholas shepherded them downstairs, and half an
hour later the deed was done. The ceremony was
completely unreal to Jenny until the moment came to

sign her new name. She hesitated for so long that
Nicholas put his hand over hers. 'You can't have
forgotten it already,' he said gently. It was real, after
all. She must learn to think of herself in future as Mrs
Nicholas Redfern.

It was easier at the hotel, with other people to think
about, and red-headed Emily was cheerfully waiting
to be recognised.

'Lovely to think you're safely tied up,' she announced happily. 'I know a threat when I see one.'

Jenny smiled but didn't deny the idea. It might
encourage Emily to exert herself on Andrew's behalf if
she thought there had been some competition around.
Andrew didn't deny it either, being lost in the bitter
thought that taking Jenny to that damned gala had
alerted not only Emily to an unsuspected danger.
Nicholas wasn't the man to let the grass grow under
his feet, or to wait for a rival to walk off with the girl he
wanted for himself. No wonder this wedding was
being pushed through with the usual Redfern speed.

Jenny had already met the pleasant, plain-faced
woman who was going to live with James at Hans
Place. Talking to her again now, she was even more
certain that Lorna Kennet was an ideal person to take
care of James without fussing him to death. They were
still chatting together when there was an irruption
outside. The next moment Arthur Ainslie surged into
the room, first as usual, followed by Joanne, with
Mary Ainslie bringing up the rear—also as usual.
Jenny went over to join Nicholas who was already
greeting them, stifling the need to burst out laughing
at the expression on Andrew's face. His gaze was
riveted on Joanne, apparently poured into a yellow
mini-dress *just* on the hither side of decency. White
fishnet tights and shiny white boots completed an

outfit which left almost nothing to the imagination. She was short like her father, but the proportions were very much better. Plumpness might eventually set in, but for the moment Jenny doubted whether a man would have any complaint to make. How in the world had poor discouraged Mary managed to produce such a daughter? She was so determined to raise the blood pressure of every male in sight that she might have ended up making them smile instead. But there was something about Joanne Ainslie that defied laughter. She was too full of vitality, and too positively a person—like her father; you might not like either of them, but you couldn't underrate them.

Mary Ainslie kissed the bride with real affection, and Arthur shook her painfully by the hand. Joanne's glance merely skimmed over her before fastening itself on Nicholas. Much to her own astonishment Jenny felt sorry for her; a girl couldn't *not* be dazzled by him. He was altogether too potently attractive, and unless they locked him out of sight for the next fifty years or so he'd go on charming the hearts out of women's breasts without even knowing he was doing it. Watching Joanne's eyes on him now, Jenny's stretched nerves were brushed by the first faint touch of alarm. This girl wouldn't be daunted by consider- ations that might stand in the way of normal people. The fact that Nicholas was apparently out of reach would only make the chase more enjoyable from her point of view. Blinking at the warning light flashing in her mind, Jenny saw kind Emily devote herself to Arthur, while Andrew stepped bravely into the line of fire by reminding Joanne that they'd previously met at Covent Garden. By the time lunch was over she had no doubt that she'd filled him with desperate desire— which was the truth, he afterwards confided to Emily, although she'd misinterpreted the nature of the desire.

'You did your best,' said Emily approvingly, 'but Jenny's going to have trouble with that one.'

'You mean Nicholas is?'

'Same thing!' Emily studied Andrew's face, then took her bull by the horns. 'Jenny's a peach, by the way; no wonder you love her.'

He was unprepared for her to be so perceptive, or so generous.

'You're not so bad yourself,' he murmured fulsomely.

'That's true too,' Emily agreed. She didn't refer again to the wedding lunch party, but couldn't help wondering about a couple who were going to spend their wedding evening, according to Jenny, going through house agents' lists. It wasn't what she had in mind for herself when she finally allowed Andrew to talk her into marrying him.

The Redferns drove back to Hans Place together, stayed in James's flat long enough to drink the tea Jenny made for them, then she and Nicholas climbed the stairs to their own front door. It was still hard to think of it as *her* home, but she must keep reminding herself that it was now the only one she had. The day had seemed endless, and she was about to go to her own room and shed the cream suit, of which she was very tired, when Nicholas stopped her with his hands lightly holding her shoulders.

'Difficult day, Mrs Redfern?'

'Not difficult exactly, but I'm glad it's over. All I have to do now is start getting used to my new self.'

She smiled in case he should think she was going to find it difficult, but he was aware of the tension she'd been struggling to hide all day. There was a moment when he teetered on the very edge of saying that their

beautifully practical arrangement was unworkable—
that they must live together as man and wife or not at
all—but Jenny moved out of reach of his hands and
the moment was gone.

'I've got tickets for the opera tonight—La Bo-
hème—unless you feel too tired to go,' Nicholas said
instead, when he could be sure that his voice sounded
casual again.

He got a real smile this time, brilliant with relief.
Even if she'd been dropping with exhaustion, anything was better than sitting out their first difficult
evening together, watching the minutes crawl by until
it was time to say good night and go to bed.

'Go and lie down for an hour,' he suggested. 'We
don't need to leave until a quarter to seven.'

The special atmosphere of a performance that
included the rare appearance in London of one of the
stars in the operatic firmament was already electrify-
ing the Opera House by the time they arrived.

'I don't approve of all this ballyhoo,' muttered
Nicholas as they took their seats. 'Give me a good
steady team affair, where all the singers know one
another, aren't trying to upstage each other, and are
on singing terms with the conductor.'

'Having said which, it'll turn out to be the most
exciting thing you've ever heard and I shall expect you
to eat your words!'

In the event Jenny was more right than he was, and
he had the grace to say so. It was a performance to
make very familiar music sound as if they were
hearing it for the first time. At the end of it they were
at ease with each other, content and attuned. Waiting
in the foyer while Jenny went to the cloakroom to
retrieve her coat, Nicholas was conscious of hope
beginning to rise inside him . . . it was going to be all

right after all. He was smiling at no one in particular when a woman drifting past caught sight of him, hesitated, and stopped in front of him.

'Shall we say hello for old times' sake, Nicholas?'

He stared at the half-smiling face of his ex-wife. It was a physical shock, like stepping on a stair that wasn't there. He hadn't even known she'd come back to London; certainly hadn't expected to be taken so unawares. His sudden desperate prayer that Jenny would be delayed by a queue in the cloakroom had fallen on deaf ears up above, because she was at his elbow the next moment, smiling at the stunningly beautiful woman Nicholas was talking to.

'My wife, Jenny ... Caroline Redfern,' he said briefly.

Jenny felt herself raked by a blue glance that calculated the cost of her dress, noted that she was content to wear her own eyelashes, and probably saw that Nicholas hadn't married his new wife for love.

'Congratulations,' Caroline said to her, rather than to Nicholas. 'How clever of you to inveigle my brute of a husband into matrimony again ... rumour has it that he was managing to enjoy himself quite well without remarrying!'

'We are both expecting better luck second time round,' Nicholas said grimly. 'Now, if you'll excuse us, Caroline, we're on our way home.'

'Pity ... we could have compared notes,' she suggested, flashing another smile in Jenny's direction.

It was the last thing Jenny would have thought of doing, but Nicholas wasn't leaving it to chance; his hand on her arm propelled her through the crowd as if the Furies were at their heels.

'Supper out, or home?' he enquired briefly when they were outside in the Piazza again.

'Home, I think, unless you're hungry; I'm not.'

It was the only thing they said on the way back to the flat. Jenny was seeing in her mind's eye a beautiful, malicious woman who'd managed to destroy the evening's happiness in a couple of deftly chosen sentences; Nicholas was aware of his ex-wife's effect on Jenny, and was asking himself why he hadn't murdered her years ago when he had the chance. The moment they were inside the front door Jenny found something to say at last.

'Thank you for the opera, Nicholas ... it was beautiful. Excuse me if I go to bed, though. I really am tired now.'

She was heading in the direction of her own room before he even had time to reply. There was nothing to do but force himself to concentrate on papers that needed looking at until tiredness drove him to his own bed. Damnation *please* take Caroline!

On the other side of the wall Jenny forced herself to go through the usual nightly routine of getting ready for bed. At the last moment she went, as always, to open her window wider and almost jumped out of her skin as the old-fashioned sash-cord split and then disintegrated under the strain. The window fell to the bottom with a crash that probably woke James downstairs. Far worse, from Jenny's point of view, was the fact that it brought Nicholas to her door in something less than ten seconds flat. He walked straight in without knocking and found her, tearful, cross, and half-way to being totally distraught, struggling to get the window up and fixed again.

'I thought you'd ... I don't know what I thought,' he said unevenly. 'Let me fix the blasted thing.'

She moved away immediately, leaving him to wrestle with it. Her flower-sprigged dressing gown was made of cotton . . . no reason to fear that it was transparent. But she was conscious of the nakedness beneath, and riven by the fear that he might think she'd wrecked the window deliberately to bring him into her room. Nicholas found something to wedge the pane with, then turned to look at her.

'It'll do for the time being, but I hope it's not going to drive you mad by rattling all night. Shall we change places, in case?'

Jenny shook her head, unable to speak to him without bursting into tears. His gaze lingered on her, and suddenly the situation between them was past bearing.

'Jenny . . . let's end this farcical arrangement here and now,' he said urgently. 'Come with me now and be my love?'

It was the thing that she'd dreaded most . . . brought about by that damned window. Nicholas had either sensed her own need, or was provoked by the events of the evening, or simply remembering that legally she was his wife. Desire rising in him was something she could recognise, whatever Gwen Marriot might say about her stupidity where men were concerned. But she had no sure guide now to a man's tenderness, especially when he was doing his best to give her the impression that they might as well sleep together as not.

'We said we'd . . . only change the terms if we *both* agreed,' she reminded him desperately. 'I didn't drag you in here to . . . to . . .'

Words failed her, and it was a relief when Nicholas finally spoke again, except that the sentences were flung at her like chippings off a block of ice. 'Don't look as if I'm about to rape you, my dear Jenny, and don't bother to lock your door. Sleep well!'

He was gone, and she'd seen to it that the 'in name only' arrangement would never be challenged again. Mrs Redfern could crawl into her virtuous bed and weep herself to sleep there undisturbed.

CHAPTER EIGHT

JENNY reached her lowest point of despair at three o'clock in the morning. She had mortified Nicholas beyond forgiveness, and nothing remained except to throw herself into the Serpentine. A saving remnant of humour insisted that it wouldn't be deep enough to drown her, and all she would do would be to bob up and down ridiculously. By five o'clock a saving remnant of common sense had also appeared, reminding her that the reasons for her marriage still held good. All she had to do was find some way of making it workable.

It was a relief to get up and busy herself in the kitchen. However much misery had to be hugged to herself in private, part of her contract was to be a conscientious housekeeper, and that she could at least do. By the time Nicholas appeared breakfast was laid, and the comforting smell of percolating coffee was scenting the air. He looked as unrested as she felt, but the tautness around his mouth eased at the sight of the immaculately ordered kitchen, and her neat working get-up of jeans and shirt. Jenny was going to enact no scenes, and last night's débâcle was to be buried under a brave show of friendly co-existence. The least he could do was behave as well as she was doing.

He skimmed through the morning's batch of congratulatory letters about their marriage and handed them across the table with an expressionless face.

'I'll leave you to acknowledge them, if I may,' he said politely. 'What a good thing you've had so much practice downstairs in writing the soft answer that turneth away all kinds of embarrassment.'

For her, the blandness was almost harder to deal with than downright hostility would have been, but she did her best to ignore it.

'Gwen says your new secretary is shaping quite well,' she said, 'which in anybody else's terms means that she's doing brilliantly. I said I'd spend a couple more mornings with her, running through the files. It might help to give her the feel of things more quickly.'

'I've no doubt she's doing her best,' Nicholas agreed colourlessly. The truth was that he missed Jenny in the office to the point of furious exasperation. He'd now got a non-wife he didn't want, and a new secretary he didn't want, and the fact that both were due to himself didn't make the situation any easier to bear.

He was on the point of leaving to go downstairs when a niggling feeling of remorse sent him quietly back into the sitting-room. His conscientious domestic executive was standing at the window, staring out, without seeing anything at all, he suspected. The defeated set of her shoulders hurt him and he'd have given all he possessed to scoop her up in his arms, but last night's rebuff had been the only one he needed; he wouldn't invite another one.

'Back for supper, Jenny,' he said casually. 'Can you press on with house-hunting? It's a rotten job to dump in your lap, but the sooner we can find something, the sooner we can get Lorna installed. I apologise for not helping you, but I'm bogged down in the office at the moment, and I have to get cracking in the constituency as well.'

She turned round and made herself smile at him.

'No problem: I can sift out some possible ones this afternoon and start inspecting tomorrow. I won't call you in until something looks interesting.'

Soothed by the calmness of her voice, he smiled more warmly and made for the door, then, on the point of walking out, hesitated again.

'Another thing! Could you try to keep an eye on James for me? I've put an embargo on more than two hours a day in the office, but he'll stretch them if he thinks no one's counting.'

'I'll count,' she said steadily.

'Thanks . . . you're a boon, Mrs Redfern.'

He was gone at last, and she could collapse in the nearest chair, trembling as if with some enormous physical effort. If it was always going to be like this, her new job would be much harder than the last one had been. The strains of the past few days, combined with a sleepless night, had left her wide open to invasion; all the fears that had lain in the corners of her mind now came writhing out, to gibber in front of her, demanding attention. Much too late, she realised that physical need was one of the things they'd completely failed to take into account. Her own body, awakened by Luke, had ached often enough to be loved again, but it hadn't been constantly teased by the nearness of a man who set all her nerves quivering. If her own needs were as insistent as that, what about Nicholas's? The memory of Joanne Ainslie's avid face came back to her. Finding someone to sleep with wouldn't be a problem, and temperamentally he was a long way from being a monk. But how, when he was supposed to be a pillar of respectability, was a married man to take advantage of what would certainly be offered to him?

Jenny stared bleakly for a moment at the vision of Mrs Nicholas Redfern packing a suitcase and letting herself out of the house . . . hackneyed image of a

departing wife. She had money enough to rent a room
and live till she could find herself another job. So far
imagination went, but it simply wouldn't contemplate
the rest of it . . . frail James shattered by her going,
Nicholas crucified by being turned into a laughing
stock. 'By the way, old boy, how's your wife?' The
question asked only because the answer was already
known. 'Surely you've heard . . . she walked out the
day after we were married.' Not even Nicholas could
carry that humiliation off. The news would be round
the enclosed world of the legal profession like wildfire,
and it would wreck his political career before it had
even begun.

She gave a long, shuddering sigh and abandoned the
vision of Mrs Redfern running away. There was, in
fact, no practical alternative to being the efficient
domestic executive she'd boasted of becoming to
Gwen. She was tidying her own room when a thump
on the front door signalled the arrival of Dolly Parkes,
a cheerful lady who'd been 'doing' for James and
Nicholas ever since they'd lived at Hans Place.

'Them stairs, ducks . . . Mrs R., I should say! . . .
don't get no less, do they?' she enquired breathlessly.
'Time was when I could run up 'em, but I'm not quite
the slip of a thing I was!'

She patted her size eighteen hips regretfully, and got
down to work to the strains of 'Won't you come 'ome,
dear father?' Her repertoire consisted entirely of
Victorian music-hall ballads, and the more lachry-
mose they were, the more loudly she rendered them.
Jenny grinned at her, suddenly feeling better. It was
no good wondering what a forthright woman would
make of the fact that two bedrooms were clearly in
use. She'd probably mutter 't'aint natchral' to herself,
but Doll wasn't a gossip; whatever she thought of the

arrangement, she wouldn't talk about it downstairs.

Jenny shopped hurriedly in Kensington High Street, passed the time of day with her canine friend at the flower stall and bought narcissus and tulips from his owner, then called on James, begging him to take pity on a lonely woman and lunch with her upstairs. He looked so much better than the tremulous old man she'd visited in hospital that she worked for the rest of the morning with Nicholas's new secretary, feeling positively hopeful. By the time she went upstairs again Doll had gone, and the flat was ordered and peaceful. Her hand lingered for a moment on the worn velvet of Gramps's chair; it was the place to which he'd taken all his problems, and she'd never known him get up uncomforted from kneeling there. Some of his own stubborn faith seeped back into her heart, and she was singing Dolly's favourite—'There was I, waiting at the church'—when James appeared at the door for lunch.

By the time Nicholas came back that evening she'd reduced a heap of papers offering mostly impossible houses for sale to half a dozen that looked worth visiting. He waved, and disappeared. Ten minutes later he came into the room changed into the slacks and sweater she was now accustomed to seeing.

'Degenerate times we live in,' he said, smiling at her. 'Instead of dressing for dinner, we now undress. But it's more comfortable this way, if you don't mind.'

'Let comfort reign,' she agreed happily.

'I rather think it does.' He looked round the room, aware that it looked different in some pleasant way he couldn't define. It was something to do with the flowers that Jenny always insisted upon, but he suspected small alterations which would never have occurred to him and which made the room friendly and beautiful. Over dinner he mentioned that he would be spending the following night with the Ainslies at Greenhills.

'No point in your coming, I think,' he said, answering the question she'd hesitated to put into words. 'It's just the rather dull formality of the local committee adopting me as its candidate; then we shall spend the rest of the time hammering out a plan of campaign.'

Jenny would have liked to ask who comprised the 'we', but perhaps it was better not to know if Joanne was going to be an enthusiastic part of the 'Redfern for Parliament' campaign. Instead, she asked a question that had been intriguing her for some time.

'Why the Grantwich constituency? Is it just because Arthur happens to live there, and you've done so much legal work for him that he knows you're the man they want?'

'I think that's how Arthur sees it, probably. But from my point of view, it happens to be ideal. Geographically it's easy to get to from London, but the constituency itself is fascinating—very marginal, which appeals to me because I don't want a walkover, or a fight I haven't a hope in hell of winning. Above all, it's a place with a mixture of people and problems; it's got everything—wealth rubbing shoulders with poverty, countryside alongside a great conurbation, and the hopelessness of old industries that are dying on their feet being challenged by a few people with the energy needed to start new ones. I shall never find a better place to make a start, nor a better companion-in-arms than Ainslie.'

Jenny digested this in silence, aware that anything she thought about Sir Arthur would be better kept to herself in future. The dubious expression on her face made Nicholas shake his head at her.

'He's one of the people who *has* been prepared to take risks. You can argue that he's a rich man and risks don't hurt him; but the fact is that he cares passionately about the youngsters who hang about street corners with nothing to do. His knighthood was more deserved than most. He pours money into new ventures that offer a reasonable chance of success not for his own sake, but simply to get others started. In fact, Jenny wren, he's a great man.'

'And I'm an impertinent idiot to have misjudged him,' Jenny said repentantly. 'All the same, I wish he were less squashing to Mary!'

Next morning Nicholas was ready to go, but seemed unusually hesitant about actually walking out of the door.

'Let me guess,' said Jenny solemnly. 'Find a house, and look after James for me!'

Nicholas looked slightly taken aback at something she'd intended as a joke.

'Is that all I do . . . give you tasks to perform? As it happens, I was going to say something quite different . . . on the lines of—"take care of yourself, Mrs Redfern".'

No one could have called it lover-like; all the same, there was a hint of kindness in it to warm her cold heart and make her smile at him.

'Well, don't you work yourself to death for the sake of the Party!'

'Certainly not . . . you should know by now that lawyers are the most prudent of men.'

His fingers brushed her cheek in a touch light as a moth's wing, then he disappeared down the stairs, leaving the flat strangely empty without him. Already it was hard to remember that she'd lived happily alone for years; now, she was used to the sight of his briefcase sitting like a watchdog in the hall, and the knowledge that he was sleeping on the other side of her bedroom wall.

She spent another morning in the office with Nicholas's new secretary, then offered Gwen lunch of bread and cheese upstairs. Miss Marriot looked round the room and gave a small sigh of satisfaction.

'Nice up here,' she said briefly. Then her glance travelled on, to stop at her companion's face. 'You all right? You look a bit thin to me.'

Jenny smiled, not over-brightly, she hoped. Whatever Gwen might say about her failing antennae, she had the eyes of a lynx and the instincts of a hunting terrier.

'I'm fine—getting acclimatised very well to my new life, and busy finding us a house,' she added in case Gwen should be wondering why she hadn't gone to Greenhills with Nicholas.

'Anything promising yet?'

'I think so. In fact, James has bravely agreed to come with me to see it this afternoon. It's in a small terrace running down to the river, just past Hammersmith Bridge. According to the estate agents, the house itself has been well looked after, but the garden is a wilderness. Sounds as though it might be ideal.'

'Sounds more like a nightmare to me, speaking as one who finds two window boxes hard work.' Gwen drank the last of her coffee and stood up to go. 'Talking of which, I suppose it's time I hounded our Mr Fox back to the grindstone. Thanks for the lunch, love . . . see you.'

Half an hour later, Jenny and James took a taxi to Barnes. It pulled up outside a house she knew immediately that she would like to live in. The small row of Victorian houses looked freshly decorated, but they hadn't been wrenched out of period with modern doors and windows that felt as worrying as an ill-fitting tooth.

Inside, she settled James in the folding chair she'd brought for the purpose so that he shouldn't get over-tired, and they studied the layout of the ground floor together. The wall between an otherwise narrow hall and the rooms alongside it had been completely removed, and the only division now was a graceful archway that hinted that a wall had once been there. Jenny furnished the front room in her mind as a study for Nicholas; the back one leading to the kitchen was obviously the dining room. The drawing room was on the floor above, with two long balconied windows overlooking the street, and pretty shelved alcoves on each side of the fireplace. One bedroom and a bathroom led off the same landing; above that were two more bedrooms and another bathroom. She refused to let James climb as far as that, but when they were back downstairs again she waited anxiously for his verdict. He settled himself on his chair again, stroked his chin, and then shook his head.

'You . . . you don't like it, James . . . don't you think it will do?'

The disappointment in her face was almost too much for him, but he looked pessimistic for a moment or two longer before beginning to smile.

'Jenny dear . . . I'm teasing! It's a charming house. If a surveyor finds nothing wrong, I doubt if you could do better.'

'But do you think Nicholas will like it?'

'Of course . . . fool if he doesn't. Let Andrew start the ball rolling for you straight away; doesn't commit you to anything before Nicholas has a chance to look at it.'

Satisfied, she took a last look round, this time with
the proprietorial eyes of the woman whose house it
was going to be, then took James home and asked
Andrew to organise a surveyor's visit and put in a
provisional bid. She cooked supper for herself with
less than half her mind on the job, while the rest of it
considered that wilderness of a garden, and wished
that Nicholas would ring. When he did, towards the
end of the evening, he sounded much more than a
hundred miles away, and only vaguely interested
when she reported that she'd found a likely house. 'It's
in a quiet cul-de-sac in Barnes . . . very pretty, with
two dear little balconies and a biggish garden . . .'
There was no murmur of interest at the other end and
she had a mental picture of Nicholas holding the
telephone away from his ear and smiling at Joanne
until she stopped talking. '. . . James thought you'd
like it,' she ended up lamely.

'I'm sure I shall,' said the courteous voice in
Greenhills.

There was a little silence, leaving Jenny to wonder
why he'd bothered to ring at all if he had so little to say.
Then he spoke again and the reason became clear.

'Jenny . . . there's a tremendous amount of work to
do here. With the Easter recess just ahead in London,
it seems to me now that it would make much more
sense to stay on for a day or two instead of rushing
back. If Lorna can hold the fort with James, would you
like to join me up here, or would you rather stay in
London?'

The enquiry was polite, but didn't conceal the fact
that as far as he was concerned it didn't much matter
what she decided to do. Within an ace of saying that
she would much rather remain at home, she remembered something that Nicholas appeared to have

forgotten. The rest of the world was supposed to think they enjoyed a normal marriage.

'If Lorna's free, I'll be glad to come,' she said untruthfully. 'Will you tell Mary I'll let her know in the morning?'

It turned out that Lorna *was* free, and more than happy to look after James for the weekend, so there was no excuse to bury herself in the flat, wallowing in the misery of thinking herself a neglected wife. The thought of Joanne sent her out to get her hair retrimmed, and she came back with several items that hadn't been on her shopping list—a pair of beautifully cut checked pants, and a sinfully expensive dress of aquamarine silk jersey that clung and flowed in all the right places. Following Nicholas's instructions, she took a Saturday morning train to Birmingham, imagining that he would meet her there. Only Mary Ainslie was there, with the young man who acted as general factotum and chauffeur.

'It's too bad you couldn't have had a weekend to yourselves, but I'm very glad to see you,' said Mary. 'Nicholas apologises for not being able to fetch you himself, but they're miles the other side of town, going round a factory that's in difficulties at the moment. Arthur's determined to stop it being shut down.'

It was a reason only a selfish woman could have objected to. Jenny smiled at Lady Ainslie's worried face.

'I suspect the apology comes only from you! I'm sure Nicholas was much too interested in the factory even to remember I was coming.'

'Not true ... he intended coming, but Arthur insisted that they had to go this morning.'

By the end of the afternoon there was still no sign of the factory expedition, and it was obvious that it included Joanne as well. Jenny thought she would have minded less if Mary hadn't looked quite so personally to blame.

They sat talking by the fire during the long afternoon, and the conversation suddenly took a personal turn.

'I'm glad you married Nicholas,' Mary said shyly. 'He's a nice man . . . always so kind to me. But I think you'll make him kinder. Ambition's all very well, but now that he's got you *he* won't want to win against every man he comes across.'

Jenny wondered if the gods above were listening to this, and falling about laughing at the idea that she could make the smallest difference to Nicholas Redfern. The thought couldn't be uttered out loud, but in any case Mary was speaking again . . . hesitantly, because she'd got out of the habit of expecting that anyone would be prepared to listen to her, but with the intensity as well of a woman who must talk now or burst.

'Other people don't bother to hide the fact that they think I'm a drag on Arthur. He gets impatient himself, and my daughter despises me.'

The sad little confession dropped into a silence Jenny didn't know how to break.

'It's true,' Mary went on gently. 'This life we lead now . . . it isn't how we began. Arthur used to talk to me then . . . tell me how he was going to succeed. I'd smile and say 'yes, of course you are, my dear,' without ever believing it. And look at us now!'

Jenny looked, instead, at her hostess. It was all very well for Nicholas to insist that Arthur Ainslie was a great man . . . he was an inventive genius, a financial wizard, a resourceful doer of good. But surely no man had the right to reduce his wife to such a state of discouragement? Jenny saw Mary's faded blue eyes fixed on her and knew that something convincing was required.

'Foolish, superficial people can think of you as a drag, if they like, but it's only another name for a sheet-anchor! Without you to hold things steady, I think there's a good chance Arthur's boat might have floated away altogether, completely out of control. He probably realises that. Joanne's too young to understand, but she may come to realise it one day.'

'I . . . can't say I've ever looked at it like that,' Mary murmured.

'Well, you might try thinking that he wouldn't have succeeded at all without *you* . . . someone to listen to him and comfort him, and provide him with a comfortable home even when he was poor.'

Mary thought about this for a moment, then brought out the last, most painful skeleton in her cupboard. 'Arthur wanted a son very badly . . . I failed him there.'

'How can you possibly know?,' asked Jenny reasonably. 'It could just as easily have been Arthur's fault as yours.'

It was a revolutionary thought for someone who'd been feeling inadequate for twenty years. 'Yes . . . I suppose it might have been,' she agreed at last.

They sat in friendly silence for a while, and Jenny debated whether it was the moment to suggest that, along with an inferiority complex, her friend should also throw overboard her hairstyle and most of her wardrobe. Perhaps it would be better to wait and let the other ideas sink in. Judging by today, there'd be plenty of time spent in each other's company during the rest of the weekend. Mary eventually took herself away, looking positively cheerful, to inspect what was happening in the kitchen and dining-room. Jenny went upstairs to change, smiling wryly at her hostess's explanation of the two bedrooms allotted to them . . . 'Nicholas, bless him, said that if they were working very late, he wouldn't want to disturb you. Not many men, especially newly married ones, would be so considerate.' She'd agreed that she was indeed blessed among women and left the subject there.

She was dressed and sorting out the jumbled skeins of wool in her tapestry bag when voices in the corridor outside signalled the return of the working party. A few moments later Nicholas knocked at the door which led to the bathroom between their two bedrooms. When he walked in his wife gave him a friendly smile, then went on calmly sorting her wools.

'Interesting day?' she asked politely.

'Very . . . more interesting than yours, I'm afraid. Sorry, Jenny—I never imagined it would take so long.'

'Not at all. Unlike you, I don't find Mary a bore.'

She spoke so cheerfully and looked so content that there was nothing a civilised man could take exception to. Only a male chauvinistic pig of the highest order of swinehood would, he realised, want her to fling herself at him, imploring or demanding his love and attention; the trouble was that it was exactly what he *did* want her to do. She had no right, dammit, to sit there looking as if she didn't care whether he returned or not. Jenny hadn't any intention of demanding attention, but she wanted to know about the factory and its likely fate.

'Mary said the factory might have to close . . . is it going to?'

'I think we've worked out a scheme that can probably save it . . . with a lot of help from Arthur.'

His voice sounded so brusque that she was left with

the impression that she'd raised a subject he was ready
to forget for the time being; either that or he wanted to
make it clear that it was nothing to do with her.

Feeling snubbed, she merely pointed out that it was
time he got ready for dinner. He nodded, hesitated
briefly, then went away. For the rest of the evening
they were very polite to one another, and charming
company to everyone else present. Nicholas went out
of his way to devote himself to his hostess, and
Jenny—quite without intending to—so enslaved the
shy, lanky man who was to be Nicholas's agent that he
didn't hear Joanne speaking to him until she got cross
enough to shout at him.

The rest of the penitential weekend followed much
the same pattern, except that Jenny began to feel
certain her exclusion from constituency affairs was a
deliberate policy. For some reason Arthur Ainslie,
egged on by his daughter, didn't want her to be
involved. It was hard to counter the fact that she knew
little about politics and nothing about Grantwich, and
even harder to know what to do with sly innuendoes
that she was uninterested or disapproving. The
contrast with Joanne was complete—she was bubbling over with enthusiasm, and already deeply
involved in whipping up supporters to do voluntary
work. By the end of the weekend Jenny knew that
their monopoly of Nicholas was deliberate. She was
made to feel like a child hanging about on the fringe of
a birthday party she hadn't been invited to.

There was only one consolation; Mary, similarly
excluded, could at least be attended to. They swapped
favourite recipes, argued about the layout and
stocking of the wilderness garden at Barnes, and
decked the church with flowers for Easter Sunday.
During the hours they spent together the roots of a true

friendship were laid, which redeemed a lost weekend for Jenny and did much more than that for Mary Ainslie.

She looked doubtful when Jenny began by hinting delicately that grey and fawn were no colours for a woman whose hair had once been the red-gold tinge of ripe corn. Delicate hints were clearly going to get them nowhere, so Jenny made her promise that on her next visit to London they would go shopping together.

'Not ... not mutton dressed up as lamb,' Mary pleaded nervously.

'Certainly not ... but we shall put a considerable dent in Arthur's bank balance and remind him of something he's temporarily forgotten—that he's got a gorgeous wife!'

Mary smiled at the idea, but her thoughts had moved on elsewhere.

'I'm *glad* Nicholas married you, Jenny love.'

It might be Mary Ainslie's view, but Mrs Redfern was becoming less and less certain that her husband shared it. They eventually drove away from Greenhills in a silence that got harder to break with each mile that went by. Jenny flogged her brain for something to say ... she could talk for hours about the possibilities of the house at Barnes, but Nicholas hadn't enquired about it and she couldn't even be sure that he remembered she'd found a house. His nice agent, William Bennett, seemed a safer subject.

'I liked Mr Bennett,' she said tentatively.

'I thought you did. It was even more obvious that he liked you.'

Jenny took a deep breath and persevered.

'Judging by last night's gathering, you aren't going to lack volunteers. They all seemed raring to go and full of enthusiasm.'

'Unlike my wife, who seems determined to have as little as possible to do with me or my constituency.'

So softly was the attack delivered that it took her a moment to be sure that she'd heard him correctly. She felt cold and sick, and hot and angry, all at the same time. Joanne hadn't wasted the hours spent closeted with Nicholas. What was a wife to do . . . fight with her over him, like two dogs tugging at a bone? Jenny sat for a moment listening to the furious speeches inside her, clamouring to be flung at him. When she could be sure of saying anything at all without bursting into tears, she put a hand on his where it rested on the steering-wheel.

'Stop the car for a moment, please. I can't talk to you when you're staring at the road.'

His eyes searched ahead of them for a convenient opening into the fields, then swung the car through a gap in the hedge. The evening silence of the country flowed in, broken only by a blackbird's serenade in the woodland opposite.

'Talk, Mrs Redfern,' he instructed her, gazing out of his window.

'I will if you'll take the trouble to look at me,' she said quietly.

She thought for a moment that he was going to ignore what she'd said, but he turned his head suddenly and put out a hand to take hers in a painful grip.

'Sorry, Jenny . . . I don't know what I was thinking of. There's nothing in our . . . our contract that says you have to throw yourself into the mucky business of politics. It will probably help to keep me sane if you stay out of it altogether.'

There was so much regret in his deep voice that she yearned to put her arms round him . . . but the regret was not for her, of course; just for a moment he was simply seeing how little private life would be left to him in future.

'I want to do whatever *you* want me to do, Nicholas,' she said gently. 'I'd like to help if I can, or stay out if all I can do is hinder you. But the impression I got this weekend was that there really wasn't any room for someone Arthur Ainslie considers a passenger.'

With a heroism she hoped the gods above were taking note of she said nothing about the impression Joanne had been trying to give her.

Nicholas's face suddenly broke into a smile. 'The trouble is, Jenny wren, that you make him nervous! You enslave everybody else without trying, but you're alarmingly stiff with him.'

'I don't believe it—well, the stiff bit, yes; it's difficult to be natural with him. But I doubt if the woman's been born who could make Arthur nervous.'

'It's true . . . he told me so!'

She began to grin at the astonishing idea, caught Nicholas's eye, and a moment later they were both helpless with laughter.

'Well, it's been an interesting weekend,' Jenny gasped weakly when they were sufficiently sober again to return to the road, 'one way and another!'

CHAPTER NINE

THAT shared laughter ending the weekend so unexpectedly was lovely, but it didn't last. Nicholas plunged back into the affairs of Redfern's again, and when he wasn't thinking about them, his mind was obviously at Grantwich. Jenny reminded herself from time to time that there was a limit to what a hard-driven man could pack into the twenty-four hours of every day. He was always courteous, and helpful when she needed help, but as distant from her in spirit as the man in the moon.

At least there was a great deal to be said for being married to a family of lawyers when it came to the business of buying a house. Andrew had wasted no time, and within a week the surveyor's report confirmed that Number 25 Arundel Close, Barnes, was in excellent shape. Nicholas spared the time to go with her to look at it, agreed that it would do, and made sure that his offer was immediately accepted. From then on she spent all her spare time there, overseeing carpenters and painters, poring over paint samples, curtain materials, and nurserymen's catalogues. They moved into the house at the end of April, and Lorna Kennet took possession of the top floor of Hans Place at the same time. James had said that she was to consider it her own, and she didn't know whether to laugh or cry at the thought of having a home of her own at last.

'I can hardly believe it, Jenny,' she said wonderingly. 'I've been dependent for so long on the whims of other people . . . now I can stay put, with nothing to do in return except take care of someone as nice as James . . . and that's a pleasure in itself!'

She wasn't too taken up with her own happiness to go and admire what Jenny was making of her own new home, and James could always be relied upon to listen and advise, but she doubted whether Nicholas even saw that the house was being transformed. She toiled on her own, with a mad determination to get rid of every sign of muddle. It was what she had contracted for—to create an oasis of calm and comfort—and it was what she'd do, or die in the attempt. The garden also had to be tackled at once if she wasn't to miss a complete planting season, and the sense of urgency that takes possession of gardeners led her into serious error: she refused a tentative suggestion that she should go to Greenhills with Nicholas one weekend.

'I think perhaps I'm more useful here at the moment,' she said wistfully, thinking of two precious days probably spent talking to Mary Ainslie.

He didn't try to persuade her to change her mind, or say that he particularly wanted her to go with him. 'It's entirely as you please,' he said with a careless shrug.

No doubt about it . . . she'd have done better to let fifty rose-bushes wither away unplanted, and tell Nicholas the truth for once; that she wanted above all things to go with him. He was careful not to repeat the invitation, and a pattern was set that took him to the Midlands most weekends. Jenny stayed behind in London, spending a lot of time with James so that Lorna could feel free to go away if she wanted to. If he wondered about the odd way his son and daughter-in-law lived, he was careful to make no comment on it. James wasn't a man to trample on other people's private ground, however much he wanted to help them when they'd lost their way.

With the house now finished and beautiful, she and Nicholas rarely seemed to be in it alone. Life became a round of political dinner parties given or attended. If not that, they entertained droppers-in whom Nicholas encouraged to stay and eat with them, confident that his wife would be able to feed them at a moment's notice. He had time, it seemed to Jenny, for everyone except herself and the people they lived among. She made friends alone with the neighbourhood, and especially with the young couple living next door, whose two small children adopted her as most favoured playmate.

Life was hectic but unsatisfying, and Jenny knew that she must find something else to do. Anne Thomas next door put an idea into her head one day, and she waited for a rare evening spent at home to get Nicholas's undivided attention for a moment or two.

'The house is finished now, and the garden's taking shape, so I've got some spare time to fill. I gather that they're very short of helpers at St Hilda's ... would you mind if I made myself useful there?'

Nicholas stared over his coffee cup at the coolly poised, elegantly dressed girl who was all he ever saw of Jenny Redfern nowadays. It didn't need James's quiet comments to tell him that she was looking more fine-boned than before; she was over-thin. She smiled at his side in the meaningless rush that life had become, but there was no time to find each other in the crowd.

'St. Hilda's?' he asked at last. 'Isn't that the home for handicapped children? Rather harrowing work, I should have thought. It's not how women like Freda Wheatley and her friends fill their spare time.'

'I know ... I *have* tried bridge parties and aerobic

classes, but I can't seem to get the hang of them.'

She sounded apologetic, and he wanted to say that he loved her much more just because she couldn't get the hang of them. But Mrs Redfern wasn't interested in knowing that he loved her, and all he said out loud was, 'Don't strain yourself unduly . . . I can think of no reason why you have to shine at either.'

It was said very solemnly, but for the first time in what seemed like countless wearying ages he was smiling at her with his eyes as well as his mouth. That was enough in itself to lift her heart, but there was also the possibility, almost lost sight of in recent weeks, that he didn't take the social whirl they lived in seriously after all. Suddenly she could talk to him again.

'I'm afraid Freda has finally washed her hands of me,' she confessed with pious regret. 'She kept insisting that I ought to take up horse-riding. I finally ran out of excuses this afternoon and, like a fool, agreed to take my first lesson.'

'What happened?' asked Nicholas, fascinated.

'It turned out to be my last lesson as well. Freda now accepts the fact that horses are something else I can't get the hang of. I was confronted by an incredibly supercilious beast in Richmond Park and after half an hour we agreed, horse and I, that we hadn't taken to one another.'

'Poor Jenny . . . a trifle stiff, maybe?'

'Aches are developing in the most undreamed-of places! I shall probably be immobile by tomorrow.'

It was so lovely to hear him laugh again that she wanted to ignore the little warning shiver along her nerves that it wasn't only amusement that lit his eyes. He walked over to her chair and perched himself on the arm of it, one hand gently drawing a line down the nape of her neck.

'Would you like me to apply something?,' he murmured helpfully. 'Massage the affected parts, perhaps?'

Suspicion became certainty; just for a moment or two he was aware of her, even prepared to forget the bargain and take her to bed. She'd have given almost all she possessed to accept the offer of massage and what would certainly follow it. But tomorrow he would go north again, and come back with that brief flash of desire forgotten and—at least in her imagination—the scent of Joanne's insistent perfume hanging about his clothes. A night in his arms and her own defences would be laid in ruins. If he noticed the fact, it would be an embarrassment they could never get over; if he didn't, she'd feel obliged to hate him for being blind to everything but his own pleasure. Somehow she must manage without such here today and gone tomorrow loving. She forced herself to stay still under his hand, while every nerve in her body responded to the warmth of it through the thin wool of her shirt.

'It's kind of you to offer, but I think the aches might be preferable to the lingering smell of Sloane's Liniment!' The false brightness of it made her wince inwardly, and had an even more obvious affect on Nicholas. His hand fell away as if it had been stung, and a moment later he walked back to his own chair.

'As you wish,' he murmured in a bored voice, and returned to the papers he was reading. He made no sense of them, because his mind was wrestling with the problem of why a man should continue to hope that his wife might fall in love with him when it was made obvious to him time and time again that she had no intention of doing any such thing.

Jenny enrolled for morning duties at the school, thinking Nicholas might be right in saying she would find the work harrowing. In fact it was nothing of the kind; among their own kind even the most handicapped children took their condition for granted, and helping to look after them and growing to love them did something to fill the gaping void at the centre of her own life. She felt real with the children, instead of the elegantly dressed doll who smiled at Nicholas's side in public.

Jenny looked at her diary at breakfast one morning and heaved a sigh of relief. 'I can't believe it ... a week without a single social engagement.'

'Not quite, surely. You've forgotten the Ainslies' party on Friday.'

'What party?' she asked blankly.

'My dear girl ... you can't have forgotten!' Nicholas was still patient, unaware of the storm to come. 'It's Joanne's twenty-first birthday ... I clearly remember handing you the invitation card.'

On the verge of denying it, Jenny had a sudden recollection of the thick, opulent envelope in her hand. Just the feel of it had been distasteful, and she'd thrust it into her writing desk for the time being.

It was a piece of Freudian cowardice that had now undone her, because she'd since forgotten to take it out again.

'F ... Friday, did you say? They won't expect us,' she ventured hopefully. 'I didn't reply.'

'I told Arthur we'd be there, of course.'

'I won't be.' Sheer nervousness made her sound defiant rather than regretful.

'Where *will* you be, may I ask?' he asked, not convinced that she was serious.

'Next door, looking after Hannah and Timothy.'

'Who the hell are they?'

'Oh, Nicholas . . . you know perfectly well. Anne's children. I promised to babysit for her.'

He stared at her across the table. 'Let me be sure I've got this clear,' he said in his most professional manner. 'Are you seriously proposing to cut a formal dinner party and dance, which I have accepted for both of us, for the sake of a couple of brats who are nothing to do with us?'

'They *are* something to do with us —they're our neighbours,' said Jenny stubbornly. 'But if you want to put it that way, yes, I am. I promised Anne ages ago. She never goes out, and she never asks favours. I talked *her* into accepting an invitation with Robert; I can't possibly back out now.'

'I'm delighted for her to go out,' Nicholas observed coldly, 'but let some other kind neighbour look after their children. If everyone's as community-minded as you, it shouldn't be difficult.'

The inhumanly calm voice provoked her into shouting at him, determined that for once she would make some impression on him.

'You don't understand . . . Tim's asthmatic. He's perfectly all right with me because he knows me. Someone he's not sure of would be certain to upset him!'

She stared at Nicholas's set face, aware that she owed him an apology, but that he owed her something too, which wasn't going to be forthcoming.

'I'm truly sorry to have made such a muddle, but I can't let Anne down now, and since Joanne certainly won't care whether I'm there at her party or not . . .'

'. . . you feel justified in offending the Ainslies and making me look foolish.'

Her eyes beseeched him to say that he understood.

Almost he wavered and did so, but some mixture of irritation and disappointment put a stumbling block in the way that he couldn't get himself over.

'Well, I must go alone in that case, and make your apologies,' he said eventually.

'Yes ... please,' replied Jenny, defeated. 'I'll write to Mary.'

The subject wasn't referred to again. When Friday evening came she let herself out of the house to go next door while Nicholas was still changing. A quarter of an hour later she saw him get into his car and drive away. She saw the children into bed, read to them until they fell asleep, and then sat wide awake and troubled until Anne and Robert crept in at one o'clock.

'Sorry to be so terribly late,' Anne whispered. 'Are you worn out?'

'Certainly not—they've been sleeping like lambs for hours. Did you enjoy yourselves?'

'It was marvellous. In my borrowed plumes, my husband thought I was the most beautiful woman there! I'll return the caftan when it's been cleaned, Jenny.' Her kind round face was still alight with the pleasure of the evening; it wasn't possible to regret letting her go. Robert escorted Jenny back to her own front door.

'Thanks, my dear,' he said gratefully. 'We'll gladly do the same for you one of these days!'

He looked along the quiet street. 'Nicholas's car not here?'

'No ... he had a late engagement. Thanks for bringing me home.'

She went upstairs, but not to sleep. It wasn't until half-past four that she heard Nicholas softly shut the front door and walk past her bedroom to his own room on the top floor.

He was due to address a meeting that evening, and Jenny knew that he'd be up and about as usual, no matter what time he'd gone to bed. She forced herself to get breakfast, felt her stomach heave at the sight of food, and sat drinking coffee while a polite stranger faced her across the table.

'Good . . . good party?' she enquired at last.

'Excellent . . . how was your evening?'

His voice was inhumanly devoid of the smallest grain of interest in how her evening had really been. She put her cup carefully back on its saucer. The little definite click it made was the sound of a door finally closing on hopes so dear and distant that she'd hardly dared to acknowledge that they were there. She sat shaken by the knowledge that she hated Joanne Ainslie. Even in the worst moments of losing Luke, she'd been ravaged by a sense of failure, but not by hate. Now, given not the slightest encouragement to do so, she'd handed the whole of her heart away this time to a man who saw her in the same light as James saw Lorna Kennet.

'You're looking tired, Jenny.' The cool voice jerked her eyes back to Nicholas again. 'The school work is too much for you.'

'I enjoy it . . . what I *do* get tired of is the round of parties with people who bore me as much as I probably bore them.' She could scarcely have chosen a worse moment to say so, but if she didn't force herself on to the attack she'd break down and implore him to love her.

'I'm sorry my friends have that effect on you.' The cold tone told her how much offence she'd given him.

'Your *friends* don't bore me,' she said quickly, 'but these people aren't friends; I can't bear to watch them trying to go one better all the time, and working out how they can use each other.'

The knowledge that he couldn't deny the truth of it lashed Nicholas into sudden rage.

'Don't go on, my dear Jenny. You've made it abundantly clear already that the sordid business of helping to run this country isn't something that appeals to you. We can't all take that genteel view.'

He got up from the table, hands driven into the pockets of his jacket in case they should be tempted to touch her. 'I must go . . . I'm picking up the Ainslies from their hotel in ten minutes.'

'Heaven forbid that we should keep Joanne waiting,' Jenny murmured, white-lipped.

'Or Andrew,' he said silkily. 'I gather that he's not exactly a stranger here.'

'You gather correctly,' she agreed, rashly determined not to mention that whenever Andrew called he always brought Emily with him.

Nicholas was across the room in three quick strides, and his hands clamped themselves cruelly on her shoulders.

'Let me remind you of something . . . you're married to me, Jenny Redfern. I'm thinking it's high time I proved it to you before some other man takes you to bed with him.'

Instinct told her that the slightest resistance would shatter what remained of his self-control, and pride refused to beg that his hands were hurting her.

'No one is going to take me to bed,' she said as evenly as the thumping of her heart would allow. 'Shall we admit here and now that our nice neat arrangement isn't working very well?' The grip on her shoulders grew too painful to be borne, then suddenly he let her go.

'Speaking for myself, I find our arrangement

intolerable,' Nicholas said with slow deliberation. His face might have been graven out of stone, except that his eyes were alive with some emotion she scarcely recognised as pain. 'I . . . oh God, I've got to go . . . I'll be back tomorrow morning.'

But I shan't be here, Jenny thought with a sad certainty, because the future was finally clear. She stood rubbing her bruised shoulders after Nicholas had gone, then began tidying the kitchen, insanely determined that he shouldn't come back and find that she'd left it in disorder. She was in her room an hour later, packing clothes, when Lorna Kennet rang to say that James had had another heart attack.

CHAPTER TEN

JENNY left the house without even remembering the half-packed suitcase abandoned on her bed. Lorna was waiting at the door when her taxi drew up in Hans Place.

'He's better,' she whispered thankfully. 'I've just seen Dr Grant out of the door. He said James would recover faster if we let him stay peacefully at home. We've got everything he needs; now it's just a matter of rest, and nothing to fret him.'

'Should I try to get hold of Nicholas? He's on his way to Greenhills at the moment, but I ought to be able to reach him in an hour or so.'

Lorna hesitated, then shook her head.

'No point, I think. James will probably doze for most of the day.'

Her tired face suddenly prompted Jenny to give her a warm hug.

'You look worn out. If there's nothing I can do for James at the moment, I'm going to make some coffee and insist that you drink it.'

They drank the coffee together, then Jenny sent Lorna off to lie down while she sat by James's bed. His face looked grey still, but he was breathing easily. Suddenly his eyes were open, and he was managing to smile at her.

'Dreamed you were here a little while ago,' he murmured.

'I was . . . you've almost woken up several times.'

'Made a nuisance of myself again—sorry!'

She leaned forward to kiss his cheek, then settled back again, holding his hand in hers.

'Nicholas will be back tomorrow morning, unless you'd like me to get hold of him now?'

James shook his head. 'Don't bother him, my dear. Whenever I see him he looks a good deal more tired than I feel.' After a moment he spoke again. 'Had a dreadful feeling . . . so strong that I woke up in a cold sweat with my heart pounding—that's when the pain started.'

'Too much cheese for supper . . . you had a nightmare.'

'Nothing like that,' James whispered. 'I was sure something was wrong between you and Nicholas . . . I saw you—quite clearly—walking out of the house, tears streaming down your face . . . nothing really wrong, is there, Jenny?'

Hesitation equals tension squared—it was a brand-new equation she could make a gift of to mathematicians; already proven too, by James's clutch on her hand. Nicholas might find their life together intolerable, but James could die if she told him so.

'Life's a bit difficult at the moment,' she confessed slowly. 'Nicholas works too hard, and I don't think I'm much of a help to him. But there's nothing for you to worry about. Promise!'

She even managed to look at James and smile while she said it. He gave a little sigh of relief, then admitted that he yearned for a cup of weak, sweet tea. Almost before she had taken the cup from his hand ten minutes later he was asleep again, mind at ease, nightmare forgotten.

When she rang Greenhills only Mary was there.

'They're out, Jenny, love. I don't expect them back

until after the meeting, but I can try to find Nicholas somewhere.'

'No, don't bother him. James is out of any danger now. I just thought Nicholas ought to know.'

She stayed at Hans Place for the rest of the day, watched James and Lorna eat the supper she cooked for them, and then went home to find the suitcase still on her bed jeering at her like a half-open mouth. So much for running away; for the time being she must learn to stay, and Nicholas must learn to put up with her. She felt very tired, but sleep was far away. Lying in bed awake meant agonising about the future; the doing of small unnecessary tasks was preferable to that. She'd embarked on dusting all the books in his study and had a shelf full of them on the floor when the sound of a key turning in the front door sent her heart leaping into her throat. She was paralysed by the sight of Nicholas standing in the doorway, always unprepared for the effect that his nearness had on her.

'One in the morning . . . it's an odd time to be doing the dusting,' he commented in a voice she hardly recognised. The cool, impersonal stranger she'd grown accustomed to had disappeared; she knew *this* tired man, whose face now seemed all bones and angles. His dark hair had begun to show a sprinkling of silver, she noticed. He looked older than his thirty-five years, and for the moment, at least, drained of energy.

'I . . . I didn't feel like going to bed. Mary should have told you there was no need to come rushing back tonight. James is frail, of course, but he isn't in any danger. The doctor was happy to leave him at home, and Lorna's taking marvellous care of him.'

'Mary did tell me. I'd still have cut tonight's meeting if she could have reached me in time.'

It was a strange conversation . . . one of them

propping up the door as if he'd fall down without it, and the other unable to get up from her seat on the floor. Jenny couldn't do what she yearned to do . . . fling herself at him to comfort and be comforted, but just this once she could allow the truth to get a look in.

'James will love seeing you sooner than he expected. I told him you'd be back some time tomorrow. It's lovely to have you home, Nicholas. Lorna and I . . . we missed you this morning.'

'Well, now that I *am* back, will you please leave those blasted books and go to bed . . . you look like a ghost.'

The roughness in his voice didn't mislead her. Concern for James had even briefly rubbed off on her. It was tempting to take that much comfort to bed with her, but something that had to be said could only be said now, in this odd, early-morning interlude.

'I was running away this morning when Lorna rang. There didn't seem any point in going on. But James must have some sort of telepathic link with us. His heart attack was caused by the fear that we were in . . . in difficulties. I had to promise him there was nothing to worry about.'

Nicholas took so long to reply that she wondered if he'd fallen asleep on his feet without even hearing what she'd said. Then he moved slightly, and the light from the desk lamp fell across his face.

'Does that mean you've changed your mind about running away?'

She'd have given all she possessed to read into the casual question even the smallest hint that he'd rather have her stay.

'I know you said the arrangement was . . . intolerable. But I hoped we could agree to prop it up for a while—just till James is stronger.'

'For my father's sake we'll prop it up for as long as we have to,' he agreed tiredly.

'If it would help, I'd be glad to do some political work for you,' Jenny murmured. 'You've got the idea fixed in your head that I'm not interested in Grantwich. It isn't really true, but there hasn't seemed any room for me. Perhaps I could do something, even if it's only licking stamps or delivering circulars.'

'Thank you, but there's really no need. Joanne's got the volunteer helpers thoroughly under her thumb, and she knows the area almost as well as William Bennett does.'

'Of course,' Jenny said quickly. She looked down at the books in her lap, surprised to find her hands clenched round them. 'Well, it's been a long day. I think I shall abandon book-dusting for the moment.'

Before she could get to her feet Nicholas had moved in front of her, holding out his hands. She put hers into them and was lifted to her feet.

'I haven't thanked you for looking after James for me, Jenny wren. He adores you, as you must surely know by now.'

'The passion's mutual,' she assured him gravely. Warmth hovered in the air between them; the possibility of shared laughter was like the flash of sunlight on water. Then her white face made him rough again.

'For God's sake go to bed—now.'

He went off to Hans Place immediately after breakfast and came back at lunchtime to report that James had slept well and was looking stronger. It was a beautiful September day, so golden and warm that Jenny had set out lunch on the reclaimed terrace at the back of the house. She gestured Nicholas to a comfortable chair, while she went on quietly bringing

out food. Nicholas stretched himself out, as instructed, and gave a sigh of relief. The summer had come
and gone almost without his knowing it. He'd scarcely
noticed what Jenny had accomplished in the garden,
much less thanked her for it. Pots and tubs dotted
about the flagstones spilled over with flowering
geraniums and petunias still, and he could smell the
sweetness of lavender and the tang of herbs in the
warm, dry air. He watched a leaf drift down from a
little tree he couldn't even name and lose itself in a
pool of gold on the lawn, and listened to the sounds of
Sunday morning around them—the hum of a distant
lawnmower, the song a small child was singing to
herself next door . . . Hannah! He remembered the
name with a sense of triumph until the memory of
Jenny's face saying she was going to babysit for her
came back to haunt him. Life couldn't always be this
sunlit, Sunday peace in a garden, but surely it was how
it ought to be?

While they were eating lunch Jenny raised the
question that had been much in her mind.

'Is James going to have to give up now?'

'I hope not . . . he'd so hate not to be part of
Redfern's. We shall have to take more work off his
shoulders, but leave him as everybody's guide and
friend. It will mean promoting another senior partner,
and bringing in a couple of juniors.'

'There's your own work,' Jenny pointed out. 'You're
going to be able to do less in future.'

'You sound very confident about it! I'd say my
chances of winning that seat are about fifty-fifty,
provided the don't knows and the lunatic fringe don't
all suddenly decide to vote for my chief opponent;
there are a couple of others who probably aren't in the
running.' He poured more wine into her glass, and

raised his own when she drank to his victory. 'Thank God we shall know one way or the other by this time next week.'

'If the voters at Grantwich *should* turn out not to know what's good for them, what then? Shall you try again somewhere else?' asked Jenny curiously.

'Unless I make a complete mess of it, I shall certainly be offered another chance, I think.' Her absorbed face prompted him to go on talking. 'It isn't just a lust for power, by the way, though I have to confess that I prefer giving rather than taking orders! It's also a question of service . . . a country soon slides downhill if its public servants are corrupt, or just plain incompetent. Let's hope the electorate will recognise Sir Nicholas on his white horse, riding to the rescue!'

They went together to spend an hour with James that evening, and Jenny went to bed thinking that it was the happiest day she'd spent in a long while. Nicholas looked rested, and they were at ease with each other again. He spent the following morning in the office, closeted with Andrew, discussing the appointment of a new senior partner and the promotion of a junior, and for the rest of the day was clearing his desk of urgent work, so that he could leave for Greenhills that evening and stay there until after polling day.

'I'm sorry not to be coming with you,' Jenny said lightly when he was ready to go. 'Are you . . . are you *quite* sure there's nothing useful I could do?' It was the nearest she could get to begging him to say he needed her. For the length of a heart-beat she thought he hovered on the edge of doing it, but in the end he merely smiled and shook his head.

'No point, Jenny. In fact, I'd rather you stayed here. Quite apart from keeping an eye on James for me, it's less worrying to know you're out of harm's way. Electioneering gets a bit boisterous at times! Polling day itself will be very long and tedious, with nothing left to do except wait, and encourage the faithful by being seen at the polling stations. If all goes well, you can come up to Greenhills on Friday and help us celebrate.'

'I shall bank on Friday then,' she told him quietly.

'See you, Jenny wren.' He bent towards her, and her face lifted as naturally as a flower tilts towards the sun. The light kiss he'd intended changed into something that drew the heart out of her body. When he lifted his head he looked bemused; it was hard to recollect that the loud hooting of a furniture van was directed at him, but the grinning driver held up behind Nicholas's car reckoned he'd been waiting long enough.

'I shall certainly be seeing you, Mrs Redfern.' He waved to the van driver by way of apology, gave her a smile she thought would light the rest of the week for her, and finally drove away.

Jenny spent the following morning at St Hilda's as usual, but instead of going home caught a bus to Knightsbridge. There was a birthday present for Lorna to be looked for, and she was in the book department at Harrods, trying to decide between two recent biographies, when the perfume of the woman behind her teased her with a memory almost too faint to pin down. She'd just succeeded in putting a name to it—Joanne Ainslie was the girl it called to mind—when Joanne's voice spoke to an assistant. It was like the rest of her, unmistakably insistent and confident. Jenny swung round to see that Joanne had already recognised her.

'Hi ... small world,' said Miss Ainslie predictably. No insincere nonsense about being glad to see her; at

least she had her father's directness. 'You look
surprised to see me. Nicholas obviously didn't
mention I was coming to London.'

'He didn't . . . but his father's illness probably sent
everything else out of his mind.' Jenny struggled with
herself, and better nature won. 'Are you in London for
the day . . . can I give you some lunch?'

'No thanks . . . too much to do, as usual. Nicholas
wanted me to come yesterday, so that we could drive
back together, but there was a last-minute hitch at
home.'

The conversation showed signs of faltering, and
Jenny fastened on the packages at Joanne's feet.

'You look as if you'd been successful—whatever it
was you came to buy.'

'The interesting one's a dress for the party! But it
isn't the only reason I came. Nicholas wanted presents
to give to all the people who've been slaving for him
for weeks.'

Unspoken but crystal clear was Joanne's opinion of
a wife who hadn't been slaving at all, and Nicholas's
opinion that she wasn't even to be trusted to do his
present-shopping for him.

'I could have saved you the bother,' Jenny said over
the constriction in her throat.

'I doubt it . . . you don't know any of the people
concerned; I do.' She was insufferably right and Jenny
was aware of hating her for that, almost as much as for
everything else.

'Your new dress is for the party, you said. Do you
mean that the party takes place whatever happens?'

'I mean that the party takes place because Nicholas
is going to win. We'll see to that. We're fighters, my
father and I. What we want, we make sure we get.'

Jenny was aware that they were talking about

something else now, not Nicholas's chances of winning the by-election. 'Bully for you, Miss Ainslie,' she said sweetly. 'But the election, at least, is dependent on a lot of other people wanting what you happen to want.'

'Leave *us* to worry about Grantwich. Nicholas will get in, and that's just the beginning. After that we've got to get some other things sorted out . . . his daft marriage to you, for one thing.'

'So that you can be the next Mrs Nicholas Redfern, by any chance?'

'Of course . . . third time lucky, they say! It's about time.'

She didn't wait for an answer, simply turned and walked away with the assistant who'd been mesmerised into lugging her parcels as far as the lift.

Jenny told herself that it would be the final humiliation to be sick in the middle of Harrods' book department. She remembered to pay for the book in her hand without looking to see what it was she'd bought. With the surface level of her mind still functioning normally she even found the right bus stop for a bus that would take her home to Barnes.

For the rest of the afternoon she wasn't conscious of thinking at all, but somewhere deep inside her a resolution was being hammered out. She could wait for James's health to improve, and then trail out of the Redferns' life with the knowledge that pride was intact even if happiness was in ruins. She could stay where she was until Nicholas made it brutally clear that he didn't want her and most definitely did want Joanne Ainslie. Or she could fight on her own account. She'd run away once before; this time she was going to fight.

She rang St Hilda's next morning to apologise for an

unexpected absence for a couple of days, checked with Lorna that all was well in Hans Place. Then she packed a suitcase, closed up the house, and set out for the station to catch a train to Birmingham.

CHAPTER ELEVEN

JENNY didn't regret her decision, but the train journey gave her ample time to realise that she hadn't any clear idea of what to do next. She took no notice of the young man sitting opposite trying to catch her eye, and stared out of the window instead, wondering whether to ring Greenhills or get herself straight to Nicholas's campaign headquarters in Grantwich.

The element of surprise was held to be important, she remembered, in all tactical battles. Mind made up, she gave her despondent fellow-traveller such a glorious smile that he dashed to the buffet car to bring back coffee for both of them. He talked happily about himself after that until the train pulled into Birmingham station, unaware that Jenny's attentive face was completely misleading—she hadn't heard a word he'd said.

A taxi driver outside in the station yard agreed to lay aside his lunchtime racing results and take her to Grantwich.

'Lot of excitement going on there at the moment,' he said, grinning at her. 'Newspaper-men falling over themselves as usual to tell us what's going to happen before it does. You know any of the candidates?'

'One of them's my husband,' she said proudly.

The taxi was held up at traffic lights long enough for the driver to swing round and give her a long stare.

'Don't tell me which one . . . I think I can guess!'

132

Posters and rosettes of the right colour led them without any difficulty to the rooms Nicholas was using, but Jenny asked her new-found friend to wait until she'd made sure he was there. Inside, among half a dozen strangers, the only person she recognised was the agent, William Bennett. He caught sight of her and walked over, but the smile she expected didn't materialise.

'You don't remember me, perhaps ... Jenny Redfern. We met once at Greenhills,' she reminded him gently.

He was abashed by the thought that he could possibly have met her and forgotten the fact, but surely something else was making him so ill at ease? She put out her hand, and withdrew it again, because his own was strapped up with bandage.

'Nicholas didn't tell me you were coming ... I'd have got someone to pick you up,' said William.

'He didn't know himself. In any case, it looks as if you had more important things to do.' She looked round the room. It was chaotically untidy, but all the people there had an air of controlled frenzy about them. They knew what they were doing, but hadn't a moment to spare. 'I've got a very nice taxi driver outside. I'll go and pay him off if Nicholas is somewhere around.'

William's face turned slightly pink. 'He's not here j ... just at the moment, J ... Jenny.'

'Well, should I wait for him here, or go somewhere else?' Nature hadn't intended William Bennett to be a dissembler, but he did his best.

'Why not g ... go back to B ... Brum for a while ... the Grand, say. It's uncomfortable here. I'll tell

Nicholas as s . . . soon as I see him.'

'I didn't come all the way from London just to sit in a hotel by myself in Birmingham. Be a dear and tell me where he is, William, then I'll go away and leave you in peace.'

She had the softest voice and the sweetest smile imaginable, he thought—and a look in her eye that said she'd wear him down in the end, however long it took.

'He and Arthur are at a small hotel the other side of town . . . it's called the Swan's Nest,' he confessed reluctantly. He hesitated about saying something else, changed his mind, and merely added that the taxi driver would be sure to know it.

She thanked him and went back to the driver outside. Ten minutes later they stopped outside the hotel and she parted company with him. She was astonished to find the hotel lobby seething with people. No wonder the driver had commented on the number of reporters. The by-election was marginal and very important, but she hadn't expected it to give rise to quite so much fevered interest. She worked her way through the crowd to the reception desk and asked for Mr Nicholas Redfern. The girl behind the desk smiled pityingly at her.

'Join the club,' she said, with a contemptuous wave at the rest of the crowd.

Instead of going away, the slight, brown-haired girl in front of her still stood there. 'I'm Mrs Redfern, and I'd like to see my husband, please . . . now!'

The receptionist was about to say that half the people in the room had claimed they were related to him, but after an examination that raked the visitor

from head to foot, she lifted up the flap of her counter
and gestured her inside. 'You'll have to come up the
back stairs. This lot are like a pack of hyenas scenting
blood.'

A young boy was deputed to lead Jenny through a
rabbit-warren of stairs and corridors to a door that
opened on to a small annex wing, built over the hotel's
original stables.

'You'll find 'em in there,' said the boy, brimming
over with the excitement of it all.

Her first tap on the door produced no response
whatever. Beginning to get irritated by the cloak-and-
dagger atmosphere, Jenny followed it with a thump
that hurt her hand but relieved her feelings. This time
the door was opened a cautious few inches, and she
found herself peering ridiculously through the gap at
the astonished face of Arthur Ainslie.

'Didn't . . . didn't expect to see *you*,' he muttered,
for once in her acquaintance with him utterly at a loss.

Jenny hadn't expected him to welcome her with
open arms, but as a greeting it bordered on the
churlish, even for Sir Arthur.

'Nicholas is here, I think; may I come in?' she asked
pointedly.

'Very . . . very busy at the moment.'

For a lunatic moment she thought he was about to
ask her to call again. Then Nicholas's voice called
from an inner room.

'Is that Mary? I'm quite decent . . . bring her in.'

Arthur's attention was distracted long enough for
Jenny to push the door open and slide through.

'Ah . . . nice to see you, Jenny,' Arthur said
belatedly.

'And you too, of course, but I really came to see Nicholas. It would be slightly easier to get into Fort Knox, but perhaps you don't all mean to sound so unwelcoming!' She stared at him, wondering whether or not to comment on the fact that his face looked blotched and sore, then something in Arthur's expression sent her to the inner door across the lobby. She flung it open, and stopped dead, heart pounding in her throat at the sight of Nicholas lying on a couch by the window. A bandage encircled his head, and his face was ashen, except for a bloodied graze that ran down from the edge of the bandage almost to his jawbone.

'Nicholas!' she breathed, 'Oh, Nicholas . . .'

'It's all right, Jenny wren,' he said, opening his eyes to smile at her. 'It looks worse than it is.' His glance lingered on her mouth regretfully. They'd parted so promisingly, but life as usual was getting the timing all wrong. He wasn't in quite the right shape to leap off his couch and sweep her into his arms.

'Boisterous, you said,' she reminded him accusingly. 'Will someone kindly tell me what's been going on. No, tell me first of all whether a doctor has been to see you.'

'Stitched me up last night,' Nicholas confirmed. 'I'm all right except for a headache and a sore jaw; Arthur's a bit battered, but recovering, and William's certainly on his feet.'

'I saw him . . . no wonder he was reluctant to tell me where you were.'

'Yes . . . well, we had a very good meeting last night—so good that some of our opponents obviously thought the time had come for some organized disruption. They rushed in the usual hangers-on and layabouts that are always available for trouble, and thereafter the meeting got very rowdy. We're used to handling that, but what we ran into afterwards was something else again.' He frowned at the memory of it, and stopped talking.

Jenny turned to Arthur. 'What *did* you run into? A brick, I should think, judging by Nicholas's face.'

'Exactly what it was,' Arthur admitted, impressed by this accuracy. 'When we came away from the meeting room we found a bunch of hooligans round the back, enjoying themselves with a few stragglers who'd stayed behind to tidy up. We waded in and were doing rather well until they brought up reinforcements. One of them aimed a brick that Nicholas didn't see coming. Fortunately the police then arrived on the scene.'

Over the constriction in her throat at the thought of how easily he might have been killed, she managed to smile at them both. 'Cops and robbers at your age! I take it that it's the end of your electioneering, at least.'

'I'm afraid it wasn't a game, Jenny. The sinister part of it is that it was organised deliberately in the hope of putting me out of action tonight. Not organised by my worthy opponent ... this was the lunatic fringe grinding an axe of its own.'

'What happens tonight ... a knock-down, drag-out fight?' 'The most vital meeting of the whole campaign,' Arthur explained. 'Nicholas meets Jim Hennessy at a meeting to be broadcast nationally, to round everything off before polling-day tomorrow. It would have been a walk-over for Hennessy if they could have stopped Nicholas appearing.'

'If? They have! Look at him, Arthur,' Jenny
besought him. 'Does he *look* like a man who ought to
be on his feet, addressing a public meeting?'

Arthur scuffed his feet and was heard to mutter that
politics got rough occasionally. Nicholas stared at his
wife's white face, wondering if she'd think the bang on
his head had affected his brain if he got up and
waltzed her round the room. Face and voice had given
Mrs Redfern away; her cover was blown. Knowing it,
he could take on fifty Jim Hennessys, an army of
hooligans, the devil himself! But still it wasn't the
moment to tell her so. Instead, he took hold of one of
her hands that had been gripped together, dropped a
kiss in the palm, and folded her fingers carefully over
it so that it shouldn't get lost. Her eyes flew to his face,
then looked away again.

'Don't fret, Jenny wren,' he said gently. 'The doctor
swore that his pills would have cured my headache by
this evening, and the constabulary will be there in
force. I shall saunter on to the platform looking pale
and interesting—irresistible to at least half the
electorate, I hope!'

His smile confused her, and the touch of his mouth
still lingered in the palm of her hand, but she was
saved from having to find something to say by a knock
at the door.

'That'll be Mary,' Arthur muttered, positively
aware for the first time in a long while that he'd be
very glad to see his wife. Peaceable Mary was heard to
say, 'Oh, Arthur, your poor face . . . I'd like to kill
them,' then they walked into the room, holding hands
without knowing it. Once Mary had been assured that
Nicholas's wounds had been attended to, she had eyes

for no one but her husband.

'Come over here, Arthur, where I can see what I'm doing,' she said firmly. Arthur came, lamb-like, and sat without saying a word while she gently bathed the weals on his face with cotton-wool soaked in witch hazel. Jenny thought he looked what he was—a happy warrior—and Mary Ainslie looked a contented woman. Her appearance was different now: shorn of the heavy French pleat she'd been wearing for years, her hair was now cut and curled softly round her face, and the delphinium blue suit bought with Jenny in London weeks back made her eyes look bright again. But what had brought her to life now was the knowledge that Arthur still needed her.

'Lot of reporters downstairs,' Mary said at last. 'They must be a nuisance to the hotel. Should we do something about them?'

Jenny doubted not that, if necessary, the new Lady Ainslie would go down alone and confront them. In the end Arthur elected to go, with Mary by his side to keep an eye on him.

'What a transformation,' Nicholas murmured as soon as they'd left the room. 'A bit of *your* magic, I think, Mrs Redfern.'

Jenny shook her head, disappeared into the bedroom and came back with a pillow that looked softer than the overstuffed cushion under Nicholas's head.

'A woman's touch!' he said, grinning at her. 'We simply can't do without it. At the first sign of trouble, we're as wax in your hands.'

'So I've noticed,' she said drily.

After a moment he shot at her the question she'd

hoped he wouldn't ask.

'I didn't discover what brought you to Grantwich
... I suppose you heard the national news this
morning ... the damned reporters got hold of last
night's goings-on.'

'I heard nothing ... I came for a different reason,'
Jenny confessed after a moment or two. 'I bumped
into Joanne in Harrods—did she tell you? She was
buying the presents you wanted to give to people here.
It made me realise just how uninterested I must have
seemed that you didn't ask me to get them for you.'

Nicholas's hand reached out to cover her own
again. 'Don't fret about the presents. Joanne wanted
to get them. She's been such a great help that I didn't
like to turn the offer down. The trouble is that she
tends to elbow other people out of the way.'

Jenny wondered if he had the slightest idea of the
extent to which Joanne wanted to elbow her out of the
way. 'Where is she?' she asked. 'Not around today?'

'There's a big point-to-point on and she's compet-
ing. There was nothing left for her to do, so we talked
her into going.'

A complicated knock at the door was interpreted by
Nicholas as a signal that Arthur and Mary had
returned. Jenny let them in, and smiled at the sight of
a laden tea-trolley that the waiter was pushing behind
them. It reminded her that she'd eaten nothing since
breakfast time. Arthur was rubbing his hands with
glee. 'Got rid of them,' he said cheerfully. 'It's a
temptation to tell them to go to hell, but it's never wise.
Nicholas is much better at handling them than I am.'

It was the first time Jenny had heard him express
the slightest doubt about himself, and her heart

warmed to his battered red face.

Nicholas drank cup after cup of tea, but ate nothing. 'Are you really fit enough to go this evening?' she asked him quietly.

She was trying so hard to look cool and sound merely friendly, but her eyes beseeched him in a way that was far from cool and light years away from being friendly.

'I'll be glad when the evening's over,' he confessed, 'but I promise you I'm not being foolhardy.'

Arthur telephoned William Bennett to confirm what time they'd be arriving at the Town Hall.

'Full house tonight,' he said, putting down the telephone. 'The broadcasting chaps have been there for some time, and people are filing in already, William says, in case they get left outside.'

'What time must we leave?' Jenny asked.

There was a little silence. Then Nicholas said, 'Arthur and I must push off in a quarter of an hour.'

'You mean you want Mary and me to come later?'

'I mean that I want you both to stay here.'

She stared at him, unwilling to believe that he was serious. But the set of his mouth was one she was familiar with; he *was* serious, and he didn't intend them to go. She turned to Arthur, with whom she seemed to have reached a kind of friendly understanding. 'Persuade Nicholas, please. We'll be as good as gold, sit at the back, and stay out of trouble even if there is any.'

All she got was a firm shake of the head. 'Nicholas is right, Jenny. We've got no way of knowing what will happen this evening. With you and Mary here, it's two less to worry about.'

She shot an agonised glance at Mary, who looked unhappy but resigned. Nicholas registered the mutinous expression on his wife's face and tried again.

'Humour us, please. At best, the meeting will be uneventful and tedious. At worst, it will be rowdy, or even a complete shambles. Either way, you're best out of it. So resign yourselves, my dears, to the fact that we're going to leave you behind.'

That seemed to be that. Jenny shrugged, apparently accepting defeat, and Nicholas gave her a glance that approved of such unexpected docility.

He and Arthur left five minutes later. Jenny sat twiddling her thumbs for the time it would take them to leave the hotel, then jumped to her feet.

'It ought to be safe to go now. Don't let me coerce you, Mary, but I'm off to the meeting. Fortunately Nicholas didn't make me promise ... he merely instructed!'

'If you're going, so am I,' said Mary.

They walked to the door like a pair of conspirators, turned the handle in vain, and stared at one another. It took three minutes' furious turning and twisting before the truth dawned; they were locked in, and the key had gone. Jenny ran to the telephone and explained that the door lock had jammed. Would someone kindly bring a master key, because it was urgent that they should be able to unlock the door. There was an odd, embarrassed silence at the other end.

'Please hurry,' Jenny implored. 'We're supposed to be at a meeting which starts in a quarter of an hour.'

Confused sounds and half-heard scraps of conversation finally gave way to the more confident-sounding voice of someone she took to be the manager.

'I'm sorry, madam, but Mr Redfern's instructions were that you're *not* supposed to be at the meeting.'

'You . . . you mean you won't unlock the door?'

'Mr Redfern made us promise not to,' the Manager confessed. 'He said you and Lady Ainslie weren't to be mixed up in any rough-house. Dinner will be sent up to you in an hour's time,' he added by way of consolation.

Jenny resisted the temptation to say what she thought of him, his hotel and his dinner, and slammed down the telephone instead.

'Prisoners!' she told Mary tragically. 'No wonder Nicholas didn't bother to make *us* promise—he'd already fixed the management.'

'Shall we resign ourselves, Jenny, love?' asked Mary reasonably. 'Arthur did say they didn't want to have to worry about us along with everything else.'

'That's just the point. If there's no trouble, there's no worry; if there is going to be trouble, I *must* be there with Nicholas.' The note of desperation in her voice threatened to tip over into tears. Mary heard it, and started to fumble in her handbag.

'Hairpins,' she murmured distractedly, 'isn't that what people in films always use to pick locks with?'

She located her hairpin and advanced dubiously on the door, while Jenny went over to look out of the window. The sitting-room faced the front of the hotel and offered not the slightest chance of escape; the annex jutted out over the stables below, now converted into garages, and there was nothing between them and the ground a long way below. The bedroom was just as unhelpful, and she was beginning to wonder whether she could nerve herself to start a small fire when her last port of call, the bathroom, suddenly yielded hope. The window was small but surely usable, and beside it, running down the angle between the original building and the annex they were in, was the hotel fire escape. She fled back to the sitting-room, where Mary was still kneeling by the door.

'This isn't going to work,' said Lady Ainslie forlornly. 'They always make it look so simple, too.'

'Don't bother . . . we can use the bathroom window, Mary.'

Jenny dragged her across the room, stopping to pick up Nicholas's car keys on the way. 'Look . . . they must have taken Arthur's car, so the Jaguar will be somewhere outside.'

She slid through the window, grateful to discover that the roof of the stables below the windowsill overhung the courtyard by a foot or so. It provided a reasonable ledge to stand on while she guided Mary backwards out of the window in her turn. Lady Ainslie, though, was made of sturdier stuff. There was an agonising moment when she was stuck half-way, incapable of going forward or back.

'Try sideways,' Jenny implored. Mary obediently heaved herself back into the bathroom and tried again. Two minutes later, flushed, dishevelled but triumphant, she was on the stable roof as well, and all they had to do was climb over the railing of the fire escape and walk down to the ground. Nicholas's long green car was parked alongside the garage. Jenny told Mary to get in, and disappeared inside the hotel door.

'What was that for?' asked Mary as Jenny finally settled herself in the driver's seat.

'Told them we wouldn't be wanting dinner,' she said with a grin. Then they were nosing their way out of the drive, en route for the Town Hall.

CHAPTER TWELVE

IT was all very well to make a game of escaping from the hotel, but the compulsion beating in her mind was anything but childish. Jenny forced herself to concentrate on driving Nicholas's car through the early evening traffic and to pay attention to Mary's directions for getting them to the Town Hall, but underneath this surface attention she was listening all the time to an insistent inner voice urging her to hurry, hurry to the meeting.

They drove round the main square twice, hunting for a parking space, and were on the point of turning away when someone walked up to his car just ahead of them, got in, and drove away. She eased the Jaguar into the vacant space, and they dashed across the forecourt of the Town Hall and up the steps. A police sergeant at the door examined them, fortunately recognised Mary Ainslie, and undertook to escort them inside.

'You're a bit late,' he murmured, 'meeting's been going on some time.'

There were more policemen inside the building; if trouble was going to arise tonight there would be more than enough people to deal with it. The hall doors were closed but, with the eye of their helpful sergeant on him, the constable standing guard let them through into the crowded room. Squeezed in among the people standing at the back, Jenny's eyes flew to the platform. Her heart missed a beat because she couldn't immediately find Nicholas, then she realised that he'd decided to rid himself of the bandage round his head. Presiding over things on the platform was the interviewer and chairman, looking self-important and intense. Facing each other across the table were the two main contestants in the election—Nicholas, and a burly red-faced man called James Hennessy. Behind them were ranged a small group of officials and principal supporters. Mr Hennessy was on his feet, Nicholas was listening to him with an air of courteous attention which Jenny knew concealed the most profound boredom. Under the bright lights in the hall he looked pale and very tired, but he'd been careful to seat himself so that the damaged side of his face was turned away from the audience. Whatever he might pretend, it wasn't part of his tactics to gain votes by playing the part of the wounded hero.

A rustle behind her distracted Jenny from the platform for a moment. She turned round to find someone tapping her on the shoulder—it was Andrew Fox, smiling at the astonishment in her face.

'Heard about last night's rumpus,' he murmured. 'Thought Nicholas might need some reinforcements.'

She gave him a smile brilliant with gratitude, then turned her attention to the stage again. It was no surprise to find Nicholas a competent public speaker, but she hadn't expected a performance as polished as this. He was handicapped by an interviewer who was clearly biased in favour of the other candidate, but, unlike the perspiring Mr Hennessy, who was earnest, repetitive, and apt to wander from the point, he gave concise answers, took courteous issue with the

chairman when a question was blatantly unfair, and
even managed the feat of injecting some humour into
the proceedings. Half the people in the hall obviously
hung on his words, and the other half began to look
depressed. Jenny was anxious and proud in roughly
equal parts, willing everyone there to understand what
manner of man it was offering to represent them.

At last the interviewer called a halt to proceedings
that were becoming increasingly one-sided. Before he
wound up the evening, he said, both candidates would
be allowed a few minutes for a final declaration of
their claim to be supported at the poll the following
day. Mr Hennessy heaved himself to his feet again, to
the fervent applause of the very large lady sitting on
his right, and Jenny belatedly took in the significance
of the empty chair beside Nicholas. Jim launched into
an emotional account of his love-affair with
Grantwich and every last one of its inhabitants. No
one was dearer to his heart except, of course, his stout-
hearted Gladys . . . cheers from one side of the hall.
Gladys had fought the good fight with him every inch
of the way, like the wonderful trooper she was. Then
Mr Hennessy waxed not only eloquent but untruthful:
he looked at Nicholas and said that he pitied an
opponent who had been left to struggle alone; he
pitied Grantwich even more if it saddled itself with an
M.P. whose wife hadn't troubled to leave London
even for this final important evening. It was Jim's
most successful hit of the entire meeting—the signal
for delirious applause from his supporters, and
uneasiness among Nicholas's ranks. Watching them,
Jenny only just heard Andrew's voice in her ear.

'I think you're on, Mrs Redfern!'

'You mean . . . go up there?' she whispered, aghast.

'Now is the time for all good women to come to the aid of the Party!'

He gave her a gentle shove, and without conscious thought Jenny found herself walking along the centre aisle of the hall. She felt exposed and ridiculous, but once started it was unthinkable to turn tail and go back. She got to the steps leading up to the platform, and had a fleeting glimpse of the emotions chasing themselves across Nicholas's face; then he got to his feet and led her to the empty chair beside him. Aware that Mr Hennessy's ace had just been trumped, Nicholas's supporters went wild, until the chairman finally managed to call the meeting to order again.

'Ladies and Gentlemen, we know that Gladys Hennessy has been a courageous campaigner for Jim; in fact, she is an old friend. But since a lady who has so far been invisible has decided to appear, perhaps we should ask *her* to say a few words.'

The conviction that whether she accepted or declined she would make a fool of herself was in the malicious smile he gave her, and in the ironic cheers coming from one side of the hall. She heard Nicholas mutter 'you bastard' under his breath, then his agonised whisper only just reached her above the noise in the hall. 'There's no need, my love.' She couldn't be sure she really heard those last two words.

'I think there *is* a need,' she said quietly. He stared at her for a moment, then pushed the microphone in front of him across to her.

'Good . . . good evening to you all,' she began nervously. 'Mr. Hennessy was right to . . . reproach me for being absent from the campaign, but wrong to assume it was because I thought Grantwich didn't matter. I was anxious not to get in Nicholas's way. There's nothing I can say that he can't say better—except this. I couldn't help noticing the division down the hall this evening. But if Nicholas is elected tomorrow he'll make sure that he represents the whole of Grantwich. I hope you'll let him serve you—you'll never have a more honourable, capable or devoted representative in Parliament.'

The declaration came slowly, from her heart. Mrs Redfern had nailed her colours to the mast at last . . . in public. The audience was silenced for a moment or two and Nicholas gave the chairman no chance to break the spell. He leaned across and spoke into the microphone. 'No more speeches, ladies and gentlemen—you've probably had as many as you can bear to listen to. You know the parties we represent, and the policies we believe in, but what you have to choose tomorrow is people. If you decide to choose us—Jenny and me—we will do our best to serve you. Good night.'

Pandemonium broke out again, and the chairman gave up the pretence that he was in charge of the proceedings. Under cover of the noise Nicholas gripped Jenny's hand.

'I ought to beat you, Jenny wren, and I shall have something to say to the manager of the Swan's Nest later on, but I rather think you've just saved our bacon!'

Arthur Ainslie joined them in time to hear her say, 'Don't blame the manager . . . Mary and I climbed out of the bathroom window. She's at the back of the hall.'

Nicholas collapsed into a shout of laughter that hurt his sore face, but Arthur's mouth fell open.

'Climbed out of the window . . . Mary did? My lass is running amok!'

'It wasn't so very dashing,' Jenny confessed. 'We came down the fire escape!' She turned to grin at Nicholas. 'More reinforcements at the back—Andrew drove up, in case you needed help.'

'In case *you* needed help, I expect,' he said lightly.

She could only let the wry comment stand as a joke, but she was suddenly depressed by the feeling that he'd completely mistaken Andrew's gesture. Something that should have given him pleasure had irritated him instead.

The hall was emptying, and Mary, escorted by Andrew, felt brave enough to wave at her husband. 'The cheek of it . . . climbing out of windows,' Arthur growled to no one in particular. He stalked off the platform to meet them, frowned at his wife, then changed his mind and kissed her instead. Jenny just had time to see her face flush with pleasure before Nicholas drew her across the platform to shake hands with the Hennessys. Ten minutes later the courtesies were over and they were free to leave.

Andrew kissed her more warmly than she liked by way of congratulation and suggested finding himself a room for the night at Nicholas's hotel.

'No chance,' said Arthur firmly. 'They've got journalists sleeping three to a room already. You must come back to Greenhills. Nicholas ought to be there too, but he insists that he's less of a nuisance where he is.'

Andrew accepted the offer, and said that he would drive Jenny back in his car behind the Ainslies. She thought that Nicholas looked poker-faced as well as very pale when he walked out to the cars to see them on their way.

'Promise me you'll go to bed now . . . you look worn out,' she murmured. She wanted to stay and take care of him, kiss away the disapproval she sensed in him. It was hard to get into Andrew's car and leave him alone.

'Don't fret about me, Jenny wren,' he said coolly. 'I shall be in bed by the time you've got to the end of the town.' He looked down at her, face white in the moonlight, mouth tremulous and eyes enormous with concern. She was much too desirable to leave about unclaimed, and Andrew's expression rammed home the fact. But their thrice-damned arrangement apart, pain was hammering inside his skull again and his face felt on fire.

'I haven't thanked you for coming today . . . I *am* very grateful,' he said stiffly.

The moment when she had been inside the magic circle had come and gone. She was wandering outside the fence again. 'Well, good luck tomorrow, Nicholas,' she whispered.

He nodded, and opened the car door for her, and stood there watching them out of sight. Tiredness, combined with too much emotion, left her struggling with tears, and when she dared open her eyes again it was to find Andrew peering dubiously at the tail lights of the car ahead.

'Dammit . . . we're following the wrong chap. I must have lost Arthur at the last set of traffic lights.'

They were now in a one-way system that brought them after ten frustrating minutes back to the Town Hall again. The person Andrew asked gave them instructions so vague that they took another wrong road, and when they finally reached Greenhills it was to find that Mary and Arthur had given them up and gone to bed. Joanne was waiting for them, and Jenny could imagine her insisting that she would wait and welcome the visitors. She smiled at Andrew, and came as close as she could to ignoring Jenny. If she'd heard about her mother's hotel escapade, and presumably she had, she wasn't going to comment on it.

'You didn't exactly hurry back,' she told Andrew with a knowing smile. 'Ma wanted to wait up, but I told her that would be tactless!'

Jenny left Andrew explaining why it had taken them so long to get to Greenhills. It would make no difference to the construction Joanne wanted to put on it, but she was too tired to care. She stepped out of clothes she seemed to have been wearing for days and fell into bed and a bottomless well of sleep. Tomorrow she must find her way back to Nicholas, spend the day with him visiting polling stations and whipping in lukewarm voters, but just for the moment there was nothing in life but this overwhelming craving for sleep.

She woke at half-past nine, fled to shower and dress, and twenty minutes later hurtled downstairs in search of Mary Ainslie. She found her in the dining room, placidly drinking tea.

'Mary . . . good morning . . . I meant to be up hours ago. I was going to ask if someone could take me back to the hotel . . .'

'Don't fret yourself, love,' Mary calmly interrupted. 'Nicholas said you were to be allowed to sleep. Andrew's already had breakfast and set off for London.'

'If Baines or someone could drive me, I won't bother about breakfast . . .'

'Nonsense, Jenny. We'll go together when you've had a good breakfast. It's going to be another long day, and Nicholas has got plenty of helpers. Arthur and Joanne went over to the Swan's Nest at seven o'clock this morning, so there's nothing for you to worry about.'

Jenny sat down at the table, with a polite smile on her mouth and death in her heart. Joanne once again was where *she* ought to be, and Mary thought there was nothing to worry about. She forced down scrambled egg and toast she didn't want, in the hope that the sooner she'd eaten, the sooner they would leave. Unaware of the fever of impatience raging inside her guest, Mary showed no signs of hurrying. There were household matters to settle, telephone calls to make before she was ready to set off. They spent the rest of the morning driving around from one polling station to the next, just missing Nicholas or misguessing his route. In the course of the morning they bumped into Jim Hennessy three times, but saw no sign of Nicholas until William Bennett told them he'd just left the committee rooms to go back to the hotel.

Nicholas was in the lobby when they got there, talking to half a dozen reporters. He finally escaped from them to take refuge in the annex wing, where the others were eating lunch. His glance met Jenny's for a brief moment, but then he was taken over by the Ainslies again—Mary imploring him to eat, Arthur wanting to know what the reporters had said, and Joanne intent on making it clear that she would be going with him when he set out again after lunch. She

talked throughout lunch about people unknown to
Jenny, plotted the route of their afternoon visits, and
discussed who should get what from among the
presents she'd brought back from London. There was
nothing, her manner said, for Jenny Redfern to do.
The constituency belonged to Joanne only slightly less
than she already assumed it was going to belong to
Nicholas. Her bright, pale blue eyes flicked over
Jenny, full of malice and confidence. It was only a
matter of time, they seemed to say, before Nicholas
belonged to her as well.

Jenny waited for a moment when he seemed to be
looking in her direction.

'Sorry I overslept this morning . . . I was full of good
intentions, but I didn't bring an alarm clock with me.'

His smile was brief and bright, doing nothing to
warm the coldness in his eyes.

'A very late night too, I gather.'

'We lost the way,' she explained, trying not to sound
defensive about it.

'Who'd have thought it of Mr Fox . . . famous in his
youth for navigating in motor-rallies!' Nicholas let
this fall with a dull thud, then gave her another
glinting smile. 'You didn't miss anything this morning. It's dull work going round, and probably doesn't
achieve much good; but if *one* does it, we *all* do it.'

Jenny's eyes were fixed on the line of stitches
running up from his eyebrow into his dark hair.

'Should you have taken the bandage off?'

'I don't think it was doing anything except make me
look conspicuous.'

'I'll promise not to ask any more stupid questions if
you'll just tell me whether your headache's gone.'

'My beauty's still a bit marred; otherwise I'm myself
again,' he said briefly. It didn't really answer her
question, but she knew that the subject of how he was
feeling was to be considered closed. Joanne, in any
case, was nudging at his elbow again.

'Time we were on the road again, Mr Redfern,' she
said gaily. 'You've idled here long enough.'

He tugged his forelock obediently and got to his
feet.

'Yes, m'am.'

Jenny ignored the girl hanging on his arm. 'I know
you don't want a procession following you around, but
is there anything I could do by coming?'

'Not a thing,' he said indifferently. 'It looks like
being a very heavy poll, so we shan't have to do a great
deal of late whipping-in. In any case it can only be
done by people who know the area. Boring for you,
I'm afraid, Jenny. Why not go back to Greenhills with
Mary until they start counting?'

She nodded and turned away, anxious not to see the
smile of triumph on Joanne's face. For a little while
last night she had felt useful to him—but the feeling
was as long-lasting as snow on the desert's dusty face
. . . 'lighting a little hour or two.' She was a help to him
in London, running his home, but absurdly out of
place in Grantwhich. The people who had toiled for
him for months resented her, and the only thing she
could do for him was not make a nuisance of herself—
not burst into tears, or demand to stay by his side. She
watched his tall figure walk away, flanked by Arthur
on one side, short and square and powerful as a tank,
and Joanne dancing along on the other. She had the
heartbreaking feeling that she was saying goodbye to

him. He belonged to these people now, whatever happened when the day's votes came to be counted.

'Let's go home,' Mary suggested quietly. 'I don't know about you, love, but I'm dying for a decent cup of tea.'

'The cup that cheers . . .' Jenny agreed with a smile that hurt the woman watching her.

They called at the committee rooms on the way back to Greenhills because Mary wanted to make sure that William and his helpers weren't going all day without food.

'Nicholas arranged it all,' he said with a smile. 'We've been eating all day long. As soon as voting ends, we shall close up here and meet Nicholas and Arthur for the count at the Town Hall.'

'If Nicholas gets in, William, it will be largely due to you,' Jenny said gratefully.

William blushed and thrust his hands in his pockets because he didn't quite know what to do with them. 'And you, Jenny—last night's meeting is all round the town!'

Jenny and Mary left him and went back to Greenhills for the rest of a day that seemed to be without end. At eight o'clock they dined off soup and sandwiches, Mary lamenting the fact that no one seemed to have been at home to eat a proper meal for days. At half past eight the others returned, tired and hungry. Nicholas disappeared for long enough to shave and put on a clean shirt, wolfed down sandwiches and coffee, and then announced that he must leave again for the Town Hall. Jenny watched Joanne get to her feet, like a puppet whose master had just pulled a string.

'Five minutes, Nicholas ... you can't go without me; you know I'm your mascot!'

His smile was very kind as he shook his head at her.

'Nothing doing, little one. You've been on your feet all day. Your mother will rightly have my hide if I drag you out again now.'

The mulish set of her mouth suggested that Miss Ainslie didn't propose to let her mother's opinion weigh with her in the slightest. Nicholas was patient with her—so sweetly patient that Jenny couldn't doubt the extent of his affection for her.

'We shall be hanging about for hours, yet, Jo, dear. I'm going to insist that you stay here for a while. If you aren't sound asleep in bed at midnight, your father can bring you down for the end of the count. Is it a deal?'

'Whatever you say, Mr Redfern.' Her voice was demure, but eyes and mouth, and her body pressed against him as she reached up to kiss him goodbye, were blatantly enticing. For once, Jenny realised, it was no pleasure to be proved right. She'd known all along that Joanne was determined to get Nicholas. His marriage had done nothing but put a stumbling block in the way ... all a self-willed Ainslie needed to spur her into getting what she wanted in the end.

Jenny thought of the mood of determination she'd set off in from London ... her laughable intention to fight. Hadn't Nicholas himself said their marriage was intolerable? He couldn't be frustrated indefinitely for fear of upsetting James's health. Nicholas needed a wife, not a housekeeper. She watched him detach himself from Joanne and say goodbye to Mary.

'Shall we see you later, Mrs Redfern?' he enquired casually.

Was the 'Mrs Redfern' intended to remind her that, for the moment at least, she was still part of his public image.

'I'll be there . . . appropriate smile in place,' she assured him gravely.

For a moment his eyes smiled at her; she was invited in from the frozen regions in which she wandered. Then Joanne intercepted the glance.

'You don't want him to win,' she flung at Jenny. 'I don't know why you bothered to come here . . .'

'Joanne! Apologise at once to Jenny. I know you're keyed up, but that's no excuse to be rude.'

Mary's distress made no difference to her daughter. She simply tossed her head and walked out of the room.

'Then I must apologise, Jenny, love. She didn't mean it, you know.'

'It's my fault,' Nicholas stepped quickly into the breach. 'I've let her get overtired, and waiting's always the hardest part of all.' He smiled at them ruefully, then glanced at his watch. 'I really must go—William will be thinking I'm not going to show up.'

After he'd gone, they all carefully talked about other things, and somehow the rest of the long evening passed. Just before midnight they set off once more for the Town Hall. Joanne had reappeared and apart from ignoring Jenny completely, seemed to be in high spirits.

They were eased through the crowds waiting in the forecourt of the building, and a bevy of reporters clustered round the doors. Counting was still going on, but Nicholas appeared from a side room to say that the result was expected within the next half hour.

Jenny recognised the Hennessys, and felt obliged to go and talk to them; in any case, even Gladys was preferable to Joanne. They did their best to keep some sort of conversation going, but as the minutes passed, tension mounted in the room, stifling everything but the unbearable need to know what was happening next door. Then, just before one a.m., the police sergeant she remembered seeing once before appeared at the door to summon the candidates . . . the result of the election was known. Grantwich was marginal no more. Nicholas had polled 15,159 votes, Jim Hennessy, his nearest rival, 11,041.

Jenny had only vague memories afterwards of the subsequent uproar, except for tiny scenes etched into her mind like cameos—rough, tough Jim gently mopping the tears of disappointment on his wife's cheeks, Arthur, white with the release from strain, dropping his head in his hands for a moment, Joanne flinging herself into Nicholas's arms with the certainty that she had a right to be there.

Jenny smiled at Nicholas's side, amid the noise and speechifying and the flash of cameras. She said something when spoken to, looked composed and happy when that was all that was required of her. No one looking at her could have known that the frail little cord linking her to Nicholas had finally snapped. He belonged to the Ainslies and to Grantwich. Memory, playing tricks, lit in her mind the lines Nicholas had once underlined in a poem by Robert Graves:

> '. . . Love went by upon the wind
> As though it had not been.'

She was just as unnoticeable . . . a balloon that had become untethered and now could drift away into the sky.

CHAPTER THIRTEEN

AT last the crowds drifted home; the endless day was finally over.

'Now surely you'll come back with us to Greenhills, Nicholas,' Mary said pleadingly. 'No reason for you to stay in a hotel by yourself!'

'It's not worth moving my stuff for what's left of tonight, my dear. If you'll allow me to, I'll come to breakfast. Jenny and I will make a quick trip back to London, and be here again in time for the party Arthur's planning on Saturday.'

Not even Joanne had the energy left to argue. Reaction was setting in for all of them. No one felt much inclined even to talk on the drive back to Greenhills. It was enough to know that they'd won, and that for the moment nothing need be thought about. They could simply fall into bed and go to sleep. Jenny was thankful not to have to shore up her end of a conversation. She had a lot of thinking to do, but instead of functioning clearly, her thoughts went round and round like a mouse searching in vain for a way out of its trap.

At seven o'clock she gave up the pretence of sleeping, dressed and went downstairs. Breakfast was laid in the dining-room, but no one else was about. She walked out into the garden, grateful to be away from the house. The morning was soft and still, and heavy with a mist that signalled the beginning of a fine autumn day. Summer was over, come and gone almost without her noticing it, and winter lay ahead.

She rounded a corner of the house, intent on making for the wooded hills in the distance instead of just wandering aimlessly. About to cross the paddock, she was brought up short by the discovery that she wasn't the only person up and about. Nicholas must just have arrived and walked round from the garages at the other side of the drive. Joanne, in sweater and riding breeches, had just ridden up on her horse and was sliding off its back into his arms. Jenny waited long enough to see her lift her face for his kiss, then turned and walked back the way she'd come, objective forgotten. Her mind was clear at last, and the relief of knowing what she was going to do even made the thought of breakfast bearable. Mary was there this time when she went into the dining room.

'Morning, Jenny. Don't let's wait. There's no telling when anyone else will come down, and I dare say Nicholas will get held up.'

No doubt about it, Jenny could have told her. He'd be needed to watch while Joanne groomed her horse, and a stable made a 'fine and private place' for lovemaking. She made a great show of eating a minute piece of toast that stuck in her throat, grateful for the fact that Mary's mind was too taken up with the forthcoming party to notice.

'Must you go back with Nicholas today?' asked Mary suddenly. 'I'm sure he'll come back all the sooner if you stay here.'

Jenny had found no answer to this when the door opened and Nicholas himself appeared. The stables couldn't have been uninhabited after all. A few hours' sleep had done wonders for him, and his face was beginning to heal. He bent down to drop a conventional kiss on her hair, and the scent of Joanne's all-pervading perfume still clung to the wool of his sweater. Jenny swallowed the nausea in her throat and got up to refill her coffee cup. Nicholas helped himself to bacon and eggs, and sat down with a glance at her across the table.

'Not eating, Jenny?'

She shook her head. 'Not very hungry . . . too much excitement yesterday, I expect.'

Mary looked at her, noticing her sheet-white face for the first time.

'I was just thinking Jenny ought to stay here. Is there really any need for her to go back with you, Nicholas?'

'It's kind of you . . . but . . . but I must go back,' she said desperately. 'I . . . I didn't pack for a party—came away in too much of a hurry.'

It sounded reasonable, and Mary wasn't a woman to try to override what anyone else had it in mind to do.

'Just as you like, love,' she said gently, and there the subject was allowed to rest.

Jenny escaped as Joanne and her father came into the room, and went upstairs to pack the overnight bag she'd brought with her. It was almost unbelievable, but she'd left Barnes only forty-eight hours ago. If someone had told her she'd been at Greenhills for a month she'd have agreed with them. Nicholas was ready to leave an hour later, and they drove away promising to be back by tea-time the following day. Gaiety dropped out of sight almost immediately, and

constraint thickened like fog in the car as the miles
dragged by.

'I don't like a non-stop conversation when I'm
driving, but there's a happy medium between that and
a Trappist silence,' Nicholas remarked after a while.
'Could you exert yourself to say something, Jenny
wren? It's your turn to dredge up a remark or two.'

'Sorry. . . I didn't realise I wasn't thinking out loud.'
The look of strain on her face puzzled him.

'Are you worrying about the future? There's no
need . . . life will sort itself out gradually, you know.'

'Yes.'

He wasn't sure what it was she'd agreed to, but
thereafter she locked in the recesses of her mind the
things that couldn't be dealt with while he was driving
a car and talked casually about how his working life
would be organised in future. Nicholas felt in his own
bones the effort she was making, but concentrated on
getting them home as fast as possible in order to
shorten the ordeal.

'Shall we call on James first?' he asked when they
were nearing London. 'I rang him in the early hours of
this morning, as instructed, and he was very cock-a-
hoop, but I expect he'll want to hear the details.'

They got to Hans Place to find James waiting with a
bottle of champagne on ice. Lorna was putting the
finishing touches to a lunch they were expected to
share. Jenny laughed and talked and ate enough to
satisfy the others, while all the time her heart was
occupied in saying goodbye to them. When it was time
to leave she went back and kissed James again.

'I missed you,' she said solemnly, by way of

explanation, then smiled because he was looking at her too intently.

They went back to Barnes in the middle of the afternoon, and while Jenny went round the house opening windows Nicholas skimmed through the accumulated pile of mail. He put her letters to one side, and left one with a Cambridge postmark carefully on the top of the pile. The house felt stuffy and airless, and she took her letters out into the garden to read. The lawn was strewn with fallen leaves, and all that remained in bloom were the clumps of shaggy bronze and crimson chrysanthemums she'd rescued from the wilderness months ago. The garden was going to look beautiful in the spring. Nicholas would be too busy to notice, but she hoped Joanne would learn to love it.

The time for talking to him couldn't be put off any longer. She went into the house to find him, but he was already already shrugging himself into his jacket; even now, apparently, the business of sorting out their own lives had to be shelved.

'Sorry, Jenny ... I was afraid the powers-that-be might insist on talking to me, and they have! I shall be expected to dine at the House, I'm afraid, so will you forgive me if I leave you alone for the rest of the day?' Something in her face made him hesitate a moment. 'Will you be all right ... you look pale?'

'Headache,' she explained briefly. 'I'll probably go and say hello to Anne and the children next door.'

'See you in the morning, then.' He made a slight movement towards her as if to kiss her goodbye, but she stepped back, and the withdrawal was too deliberate not to be noticed.

'I'm not sure why I bother to apologise for leaving you,' he said drily. 'My impression is that you prefer it when I'm not here. Character-building, but painful!'

She found nothing to say, and after a moment he shrugged and went away. Jenny spent the rest of the afternoon combing the local papers for advertisements for rented accommodation. At last she found what she was looking for: a bed-sitting-room and bathroom being offered by a retired civil servant, Miss Smythe, at Roehampton. She rang and asked to see the house immediately, and ten minutes later was taking a bus to Roehampton. Miss Smythe's house was neat and spotless; she herself was a dry, astringent lady whose only unlikely quirk appeared to be the affection she lavished on a parrot called Oswald.

She insisted on making tea for them both, and in the course of drinking it looked curiously at Jenny.

'My friends tried to talk me out of doing this in case I landed myself with someone I didn't like but couldn't get rid of. I'm doing it because the house is too big for one woman now that my mother is dead. Should you mind telling me why you're doing it? Why do you need somewhere to live in such a hurry?'

'I'm leaving my husband,' Jenny said baldly. 'I hope that doesn't put you off having me here. Our marriage hasn't worked, but he admits that as readily as I. In any case there's someone else he now wants to marry. He's a lawyer, so it can all be settled quite ... painlessly.' The word uttered itself calmly, leaving her marvelling at the ironies of which the English language was capable.

Millicent Smythe looked at the face of the girl sitting opposite her and finally made up her mind.

'Come whenever you like . . . tomorrow, if need be. We'll have a month's trial to see if we can live together.'

They shook hands on the agreement, and Jenny went back to Barnes feeling less desperate. She had somewhere to live, and, most important of all, it was near enough to St Hilda's to enable her to go on working there. That routine would hold the pieces of her life together, and somehow she could wait for a new pattern to emerge. There was nothing that couldn't be lived through, and if she ever felt like whining, the children at St Hilda's would shame her into cheerfulness.

She spent the rest of the evening packing clothes, and as many books as she couldn't bear to leave behind and, much to her surprise, went to bed at last to sleep the sleep of exhaustion.

Waiting for Nicholas to appear for breakfast next morning, she felt calm but slightly sick.

'We must leave about half past two this afternoon,' he said, sitting down. 'Until then, I'm afraid I must put in some time at the office; things are piling up there.' She was silent for so long that he looked across at her, suddenly moved to gentleness. 'It won't always be like this, I promise, Jenny. Life will get back to normal.'

She could feel the icy waters lapping about her feet. There was nothing to do but take a deep breath and dive in to them.

'It doesn't concern me any longer how life is. I shan't be coming with you this afternoon.'

His dark brows snapped together in a frown, but he made a great effort not to storm at her, even though he was irritated by an unusual display of pettiness.

'I've said I'm sorry, but we can't *not* go to Mary's party. It's being given for us, after all.'

'It's being given for you. No one will even notice whether I'm there or not. But that's a detail. The point is that I can't bear our life any longer . . . the time has come to dismantle the famous "arrangement".'

The flat despair in her voice finally convinced him that she was serious. She wasn't just tired, or piqued by Joanne's rudeness. Jenny wren was actually threatening to walk out of his life.

'I thought we agreed for a number of good reasons— James's health among them—that we'd go on as we were.' Fear made him sound stiff, and icily rational.

'I know what we agreed, but I can't bear it any longer,' she said simply. 'You or Lorna must find some gentle way of breaking to James the news that our odd marriage is over. Your political career is safely launched; a divorce can't hurt you now. Then you'll be free to make the marriage you want.'

'Is this all intended for my benefit, or do you have plans of your own in mind? The thought occurs because I couldn't help noticing a letter with a Cambridge postmark.'

It had come harmlessly enough from Gramps's friendly solicitors, but it was a gift from Heaven; she couldn't confess that all she had in mind was to move into a bedsit ten miles away.

'I'm going back to Cambridge,' she muttered, hoping that God would forgive her for the lie. 'I can hardly believe it . . . but Luke says . . . things are going to work out after all.' Her trembling voice sounded to Nicholas's ears as if she could hardly bear to think about the happiness ahead.

'Luke married someone else, I thought.'

'So did I,' Jenny pointed out, unarguably.

'You want a divorce, I take it . . . an annulment, rather, since we might as well be accurate. Let's hope friend Luke hasn't changed his mind again by the time you've got it.'

Her face whitened at the deliberate cruelty, but Nicholas was struggling with pain of his own, and not minded to be gentle with her. 'You must admit he's not a very constant lover, Jenny wren.'

'I rely on Redfern, Redfern & Fox to know how to speed things up,' she murmured. 'Anyway, Joanne will see to it that you don't waste any time.'

'So she will . . . I'd forgotten that,' he said oddly.

'I'm not sure where I shall be, but my grandparents' solicitors in Cambridge, Perkins & Warburton, will be able to contact me. I'd like to send for my things eventually.'

That sad little phrase was more than he could bear. Heroic calm went out of the window. 'This is damned nonsense, Jenny,' he shouted at her. 'I refuse to talk about it any more now; we'll discuss it calmly when I get back.'

He loped out of the room and, five minutes later, left the house. The worst was over, she told herself. Her mind skimmed over the thought that he'd gone without even saying goodbye. What had she expected—his blessing, a character reference, or a vow of eternal friendship? Still calm, she tidied the kitchen with the mechanical thoroughness of a robot, brought her suitcases down to the hall, and telephoned for a taxi.

When Nicholas returned the house was empty. Jenny was at Roehampton with Miss Smythe, installed in the room that was going to be her home. While numbness kept her free from pain, she was writing to Perkins & Warburton to explain why she was going to use them as a mailing address in future.

CHAPTER FOURTEEN

IT was almost Christmas. Nicholas had survived his first session of Parliament, and made a maiden speech that had woken the back benches and stirred the front ones to enthusiasm. His own view of the past three months was that they'd remain in his memory as the first three lived through without Jenny. He spent the mornings working in Hans Place as usual, the afternoons and evenings at Westminster, and most weekends at Grantwich. Personal life was non-existent, and he preferred it that way. Incessant activity at least made time pass, even if he felt like a dead man going through the motions of being alive.

Gwen Marriot thought she'd greatly preferred the old Nicholas to this aloof, controlled stranger who spoke no harsh word to anybody but whose eyes had forgotten how to laugh. There was no way of saying so, because he'd acquired an outward veneer of indifference that defied sympathy or question. Then she went into his room unexpectedly one morning and caught him staring out of the window in bleak despair.

'Nicholas . . . couldn't you get away for a bit? You look awful.'

Her voice was gentle for once, and she was too old a friend to snub.

'Away on my own? No thanks, Gwen. Not my idea of fun at all.'

'Since when were you short of friends—not to

mention women falling over themselves to keep you company?'

'There's the rub . . . I don't want "women". I just need to know that one elusive girl is all right somewhere.'

'You said . . . I thought you said Cambridge. Wasn't Jenny going back there?'

'*She* said that. I won't bore you with the details, but I'm almost certain she didn't go. I finally tracked down the man she'd once been going to marry. I believe him when he says he hasn't seen her from the day she left Cambridge to this.'

'I don't understand, then . . . why did she disappear?'

'Simple, my dear,' Nicholas said harshly. 'She couldn't stand living with me any longer. I could accept that, somehow. What destroys me is not knowing whether she's all right or not.'

Gwen couldn't doubt that some terrible compulsion had sent Jenny away, but it was hard not to hate her for inflicting this sort of torment on Nicholas. She chose her words carefully, then said, 'You probably won't be comforted by anything I say, but I'm sure of this: Jenny's a survivor. She'll have dug a little hole for herself somewhere.'

'A hole? God damn it, Gwen, she wanted a *home*!' he suddenly shouted. 'She had a genius for making one. What I have without her is an expensive piece of real-estate, comfortably furnished and utterly dead.'

After a little while Gwen ventured another question. 'No clue as to where she is?'

'No . . . except that I assume she didn't stay in London. She didn't enjoy city life. But my only hope of communicating with her is through a firm of solicitors in Cambridge.'

There seemed to be nothing more to say on the subject of Jenny Redfern. 'How's James?' Gwen asked instead. 'Haven't seen him down here for ages.'

'He's bearing up ... bearing *me* up, I think,' Nicholas said with a rueful smile. 'Well, thank God it's Christmas. Even the newest and most devoted M.P. is allowed time off. Sorry to have bent your ear, Gwen.'

'Any time.' She smiled at him and went away, and Redfern's offices closed at lunchtime on Christmas Eve. Nicholas arranged to share Christmas dinner with James and Lorna, and then went home to Barnes feeling as if he'd been running all his life in some never-ending marathon.

He ate without appetite or relish the food Dolly had left for him as usual, then settled down in his study with a House of Commons report, dull enough, he hoped, to send him to sleep. He never went into the drawing-room upstairs because it spoke more vividly of Jenny than any other room in the house. He was still reading, still unfortunately wide-awake, when the sound of carol singers outside in the street was followed by a thump on the front door. It was a temptation to ignore it. He felt bitterly at odds with Christmas, completely at variance with any possibility of peace or goodwill. Then a last-minute feeling of shame sent him hurrying to the door. A surprisingly small child stood there, gap-toothed and smiling.

'Happy Christmas,' he said, rattling his collecting box. 'St. Hilda's ... 'andicapped children ... they need a lotta things.'

He looked doubtful at the note Nicholas folded and stuffed into the box. 'Can't give no change.'

'I don't want any. A merry Christmas to you.'

Nicholas closed the door and leant against it feeling as if he'd just been struck by a thunderbolt. St Hilda's . . . *St Hilda's!* Why had it never occurred to him that Jenny might still be working there? With everything else falling apart, wouldn't she have been likely to hang on to the one thing that she loved doing above all? It took him five agonising minutes to find the number in the telephone book. Several more elapsed while the number rang and rang. The children *lived* there, dammit; somebody must be there to answer. Somebody was, eventually.

'Mrs Redfern? I'm afraid you're much too late. Jenny's gone,' a voice said cheerfully.

He felt sick with despair, overwhelmed by the extent to which he'd been counting on finding her.

'You . . . you couldn't possibly tell me where she's gone? I need to get in touch with her.'

'No . . . but she'll be here tomorrow morning.'

'Tomorrow?' Nicholas transferred the telephone from one clammy hand to the other.

'She'll be here at nine o'clock as usual . . . insisted on coming, bless her, even though it's Christmas.'

He supposed afterwards that he thanked her politely and said goodbye. He picked up the telephone again to ring James, and put it down again. Nothing had changed, except that he now knew where Jenny was. He got to St Hilda's at half past eight the next morning, surprised to find that Christmas had become white overnight. It had snowed heavily enough to lay a glistening coat over everything. The gardens around

St Hilda's were unviolated and beautiful. He parked the car carefully in case the sight of it should send her back into hiding, then sat and waited. She came into view almost immediately, hurrying, then stopping suddenly because the world looked so beautiful.

'Hello, Jenny wren.' The quiet voice behind her made her spin round.

'Nicholas . . .'

'You've got snowflakes in your hair again.'

They were enclosed in a white, silent world . . . the only two people left alive, perhaps. Jenny strove to find something commonplace to say.

'I read about your maiden speech . . . congratulations!'

'I discovered that you *didn't* go to Cambridge, but I've only just tumbled where you were. There's a lot to talk about.'

'Not now . . . I've got to help with the children.'

'Can I come too? There must be something I can do.' She smiled and gestured him inside. He would surely find some reason to leave again after half an hour. She could smile and look unconcerned for as long as that; he would presumably mention that their divorce was now in hand, perhaps wish her a happy Christmas, then leave her to get over the pain of seeing him again. She was wrong. He was still there when she was ready to leave at tea-time, having unwrapped presents, fed some of the most disabled children, talked to them, played with them, and lost his heart to them. Throughout the day he made no attempt to talk to her privately; he simply smiled when their eyes met and then went on with what he was doing. When it was time to leave he promised that he'd come again, taking no notice of the protest in her eyes that said the children would remember the promise even though he did not.

Outside in the snowy dusk he took her hand and led her to the car.

'It's been a long day . . . time I was going home,' she said hesitantly.

'It's not over yet. Get in, Jenny.'

It seemed impossible not to do as she was told. 'Where . . . where are we going?'

'Home, you said!'

They drove in silence through the empty streets and stopped outside the house in Barnes. How odd, she thought, that it should still look just the same; *something* should have changed because she was no longer there. Perhaps something *was* different: there were Christmas cards simply heaped on a table, no flowers anywhere, no sign that the day was supposed to be a celebration of joy.

'Sorry it looks so bare,' Nicholas said, noticing her glance round. 'Dolly does her best, but she only reckons to keep me clean and tidy . . . decent, she calls it! '

Jenny nerved herself for the question she could hardly bear to ask.

'How is James?'

'Missing you . . . otherwise all right. He and Lorna are preparing Christmas dinner for us all this evening.'

He saw her eyes go to her grandfather's chair.

'Dolly takes great care of it . . . she regards it as " 'oly," she tells me. You took your grandparents' photographs, but I've been waiting for you to have these other precious things collected.'

'Yes . . . I don't like being without them, but I'm not settled again yet. If you wouldn't mind keeping them a bit longer, I'd be grateful.'

Her hand lingered on the chair, and the thinness of it made him speak roughly.

'Tell me where you are, Jenny. I refuse to go on playing this ridiculous game of hide and seek.'

'I'm sharing a house at Roehampton—it belongs to Millicent Smythe, and a very handsome chap called Oswald. Millicent's a retired Civil Servant, pernickety but kind, and in general rather anti-men.'

'How did Oswald get through the net?'

'Oswald's an African Grey—a parrot, that's to say.'

'I'm glad you mentioned it.' The polite comment made her smile, she caught his eye, and suddenly they were helpless with laughter, not strangers any more.

Jenny mopped her eyes at last, aware that she could now talk naturally to him again.

'Lovely to be silly again . . . life is quite pleasant at Roehampton, but it isn't full of riotous mirth. Thirty years in the Inland Revenue department have left Millicent with a rather jaundiced outlook! She puts me in mind of Gwen . . . not so funny, but with the same kind heart beneath a gritty exterior.'

'If you're about to enquire after Miss Marriot's welfare, I can assure you she's as usual—likewise Andrew, Emily, Lorna, all the Ainslies, and everyone else I can think of.'

It left them very little to talk about that could safely be said. Jenny thrust trembling hands into the pockets of her skirt, and risked a glance at Nicholas because he was occupied with pouring sherry into glasses. The thread-like white scar where his head had been stitched showed clearly against his brown skin; the rest of the damage had long since healed, but his face looked taut and strained. He didn't look happy, and above all things she wanted him to be at peace and happy. The things that couldn't safely be said could, she found, be said after all.

'I've been waiting to hear about the divorce, Nicholas. When I asked Perkins & Warburton about it a little while ago they said you'd written to say you were doing nothing about it for the time being.'

'It was the only hope I had of flushing you out of hiding. As long as I had something you wanted—your freedom—I thought you might bring yourself to get in touch with me again.'

He spoke pleasantly, but she was aware of a core of resentment in him. Pride had been hurt too much for him to forgive her for running away. It was odd, and irrational, and unfair, but a man's self-esteem was the point at which he was most vulnerable.

'I'm sorry if I was childish. At the time it seemed very necessary to get away. I'm calmer now and I can see that it must have looked very melodramatic.'

She was altogether too calm, he thought—still feeling irrational and unfair. Gwen had called her a survivor, and she was right as usual. Jenny might have been desperate to get away, but she was at peace again now . . . doing a damn sight better without him than he was managing to do without her. He'd found her again, but for all the good it was going to do him, he needn't have bothered. If she'd been running away to Luke Armitage, or Andrew even, he thought he could have borne it better, felt less discarded. But not even

to be able to outweigh a feminist civil servant and an
African Grey was enough to incite a man to violence.
As if she saw the gleam in his eye, Jenny casually
walked round the back of Gramps's prie-dieu, and just
at that moment Nicholas was deflected by the sharp
ping of the telephone.

'James . . . good evening. Sorry I didn't ring earlier,
but I've had a very busy day . . . busy, I said . . . yes, I
know it's Christmas Day. Of course I'm still coming to
dinner. If the duck will stretch to another guest, I'll
bring a visitor with me. See you in half an hour.'

Nicholas put the telephone down and let the silence
settle.

'What about it, Jenny wren? Will you forget "old
unhappy far off things" to the extent of coming with
me to see James?'

At least he'd managed to disturb her at last. Mrs
Redfern's face was calm no longer.

'I . . . I don't think it's wise, much as I should love to
see him,' Jenny said desperately. 'In any case,
Millicent will be wondering where I've got to . . .'

'Damn Millicent, Jenny, and if you're about to tell
me that Oswald can't do without you for an hour or
two, I shall go completely berserk and beat you.'

'Very well, I'll come. But if James is upset you'll
have only yourself to blame.'

'It's *not* seeing you that upsets him . . . take my word
for it, Jenny wren.'

She was convinced in spite of herself by the
conviction in his deep voice. Another sip of sherry put
fresh heart into her and enabled her to bewail the fact
that she must go out to dinner in her working clothes.
Nicholas surveyed her from head to foot with a

thoroughness that made her blush. Even after a day spent with the children she was neat as usual.

'You look like the spirit of Christmas to me,' he said at last consideringly. 'I like those holly colours together.' The green and red plaid of her skirt and the matching red of her sweater looked gay and beautiful.

She went upstairs to wash and renew make-up and perfume, which was the best she could do, and ten minutes later they were in the Jaguar again, heading towards Hans Place.

Lorna burst into tears at the sight of her, and Jenny and James stood hugging each other as if they'd been separated for years.

'Don't get too excited, my dears,' Nicholas suggested blandly. 'Our wandering lamb isn't back in the fold for good. I've only shanghaied her for an hour or two.'

James looked from one to the other of them and for some reason didn't seem unduly cast down by the warning.

'Then we must make the most of her while we've got her,' he said gently.

The duck did stretch without any difficulty, and Lorna bloomed under the appreciative chorus of praise. She remembered previous Christmases spent with an irritable, spiteful old woman and wondered what she'd done to deserve her present happiness. It was she who unthinkingly switched the conversation to the subject of the Ainslies, and particularly to Joanne.

'Have you heard how she's getting on, Nicholas?' she asked casually.

'Loving it, apparently. Arthur says she's having a good time, but working very hard as well.' He turned to Jenny with a face that was absolutely expression-less. 'Joanne's over in New York ... taking a very high-powered course in business management. She's her father's daughter, so you can be sure she's applying herself as well as setting all the male students by the ears.'

'How ... how long is that going on?' asked Jenny in a voice she didn't recognise.

'Three years ... unless she decides to snaffle the heir to some fortune or other.'

'I thought you wanted to snaffle her yourself.' The words said themselves, dropping into a well of silence so intense that no one even seemed to be breathing in the room. She went red and then deathly white, thinking that a long day had affected her brain. Nicholas, when she risked a lightning glance at him, was staring down at the table, apparently lost in contemplation of the ripe Renoir beauty painted on his place mat.

'Why should you have thought that, I wonder?' he asked conversationally of no one in particular. 'I already had a perfectly good wife of my own.'

Jenny had the extraordinary feeling that James and Lorna had made themselves bodiless; still there, sitting at the table, they had withdrawn so far from the blood-spattered arena in which she and Nicholas confronted each other that it was as if they were not in the room at all.

'You didn't have a wife; you had a housekeeper and a respectable public front. That's what I couldn't bear in the end, Nicholas ... the sham and the feeling that you wanted to be free to marry Joanne. That's why I ran away.'

The truth was out at last, and she didn't even mind James and Lorna knowing as well as Nicholas. She'd owed it to them all.

He wrenched his gaze away from the table mat and stared at her with eyes brilliant with relief and laughter, and something else she didn't dare put a name to.

'I've never had the slightest intention of marrying Joanne, and any deception about our marriage is easily remedied, Jenny wren. That is enough for everybody to be going on with ... the rest of this conversation will be conducted in private in due course.'

Lorna came out of her self-imposed trance and served Christmas pudding and mince pies, and James sacrificed his best and oldest brandy to an evening which had become a golden web of happiness spun out of shared delight. They were settling themselves with coffee round the fire when Nicholas murmured in Jenny's ear, 'What time does Millicent retire for the night?'

'Soon, normally,' she said, looking at her watch. 'Why?'

'Perhaps it would be considerate to ring now and tell her not to expect you back tonight.'

'But I *am* going back.'

'No, you're not.'

Their eyes locked for a moment, and when Jenny managed to look away she knew that, however the night ended, it had to be lived through, not run away from yet again. They left at midnight and by rights she should have been half-dead with fatigue, but every nerve in her body seemed to be tingling with its own insistent life. Nicholas drove home fast, and without saying a word, but the electric tension spread like fire between them. Then they were watching each other across the width of his study, like fencers waiting for the signal to engage. Their eyes met with the hiss of sword blades meeting, and Nicholas lunged immediately.

'Why did you let me think you were going back to Luke Armitage?'

'Partly vanity, I suppose,' Jenny said honestly. 'I didn't want you to think I had nothing better to run to than a bedsitting-room on my own. But I also wanted you to feel you could . . . enjoy Joanne without a guilty conscience about me.'

He grimaced at the word she'd chosen so carefully. Even if it hadn't been intended to make him feel at fault, it had certainly succeeded.

'Is she really all right, Nicholas? I felt so sure she was in love with you.'

'Yes, she's all right, but I don't feel very proud of myself. To begin with it was simply a teenage crush on someone much older than herself—a standard part of growing up. But I allowed it to get out of hand, because I was frustrated at making so little progress with you. I fell into the trap of feeling flattered, and I was even foolish enough to think she might make you jealous. I've spent the last three months presenting myself as an irritable, burnt-out uncle-figure that she could discover herself to be bored with . . . not so far from the truth, either, if it comes to that. Mary, bless her, came up with the brilliant idea of New York, and it seems to be putting the finished touches to Joanne's disenchantment with a poor old fellow called Nicholas Redfern!'

He saw Jenny struggling with a desperate desire to laugh.

'What's so amusing about my cautionary tale?'

'The idea that you could be burnt out or boring! You've only got to walk into a room to bring every woman in it to life. They all either want to mother or vamp you, or have you trample on them.'

Even as the words left her mouth she knew that she'd said the wrong thing again.

'Every woman but you, apparently,' he said slowly. She didn't answer, and he insisted, 'Isn't that right, Jenny?'

He hadn't made the slightest move to touch her, but his eyes held her suspended in space. She was well out of reach of solid ground, no safety net below her, nothing to break her fall if he let her drop now.

'It isn't right,' she confessed quietly. 'I'd made up my mind to leave Redfern's when you asked me to marry you, because I needed to be more than just your right hand. I should never have agreed to the arrangement when I knew that it was one-sided from the very beginning. I longed for you to love me back, but I was so terrified that you'd guess and feel obliged to . . . to pretend, that I backed away whenever you came near me.'

'You mean that's been the case since the night we were married?'

'Yes, but it wasn't your fault,' she insisted desperately. 'I'm only telling you now to make you understand why it hurt so much when there seemed to be no room for me at Grantwich. The night of the

meeting I thought it was going to be all right . . . just
for a little while. Then you froze me out again and
Joanne trampled me in the mud.'

His face was so sombre that she felt she'd have done
better to leave her confession unspoken. 'It's all right
now,' she assured him quickly. 'I love working at St
Hilda's, and I'll probably find myself another flat
before long . . .'

'It *isn't* all right,' he interrupted furiously. 'It's
absolute madness. When you came to Grantwich that
afternoon I was almost sure the impression you'd been
giving for months of a half-way friendly snow-maiden
was false. I couldn't be sure, in case that bang on the
head was playing tricks with me, but then you seemed
to be telling Grantwich what you hadn't told me.
Euphoria was setting in nicely when Andrew turned
up, and gave himself away every time he looked at
you. Joanne rubbed salt in the wound by pointing out
what I could see easily enough for myself, and she was
careful to tell me how long it had taken you both to get
back to Greenhills that night. By that time I was
becoming aware that I'd made a serious mistake with
Joanne, but before I could do anything about it my
small brown wren had upped and flown away.'

His voice stopped suddenly and Jenny heard
nothing in the silent room except the beating of her
own heart.

'The last three months have been dreadful . . . like
being half alive. Have they been anything like that for
you?' he asked at last.

'Just like that,' she admitted gently.

'Dear God . . . we pass for intelligent people! What
sort of mess do you suppose fools make of their lives?'

'No mess at all, perhaps. They simply rely on instinct.'

'Well, instinct is now telling me that it's high time I closed the gap between us.'

He was across the room in three long strides and she was held within the circle of his arms.

'I love you past bearing . . . have done since you almost knocked me flying on a snowy January day. Will you be my wife now, till death us do part?'

Her transfigured face answered him, but what she said was, 'Well, it's a wrench to give up Oswald but . . .'

That was as far as she got before his arms tightened and his mouth found hers. Delight damned up for lonely months and years invaded and overwhelmed them, left them murmuring soft words between even more urgent kisses. Nicholas lifted his head at last and smiled at her. 'I've got to say it just once!

"'. . . say I'm weary, say I'm sad,
Say that health and wealth have missed me,
Say I'm growing old but add
Jenny kissed me."'

Then he scooped her up in his arms. 'It's a good thing we're married, Mrs Redfern, because I can now, in the most respectable fashion imaginable, take you upstairs to bed!'

 **Harlequin Romance**

Coming Next Month

Available in October wherever paperback books are sold, or
through Harlequin Reader Service.

In the U.S.
901 Fuhrmann Blvd.
P.O. Box 1397
Buffalo, N.Y. 14240-1397

In Canada
P.O. Box 603
Fort Erie, Ontario
L2A 5X3

**For the millions who can't read
Give the Gift of Literacy**

**One out of five adults in North America
cannot read or write well enough
to fill out a job application
or understand the directions on a bottle of medicine.**

**You can change all this by joining the fight
against illiteracy.**

For more information write to:
Contact, Box 81826, Lincoln, Neb. 68501
In the United States, call toll free: 1-800-228-8813

**The only degree you need
is a degree of caring**

LIT-A-1R

ATTRACTIVE, SPACE SAVING BOOK RACK

Display your most prized novels on this handsome and sturdy book rack. The hand-rubbed walnut finish will blend into your library decor with quiet elegance, providing a practical organizer for your favorite hard-or soft-covered books.

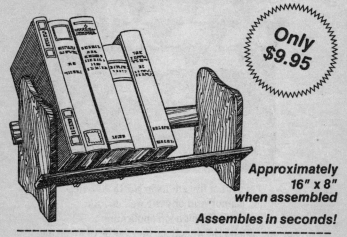

Only $9.95

Approximately 16" x 8" when assembled

Assembles in seconds!

To order, rush your name, address and zip code, along with a check or money order for $10.70* ($9.95 plus 75¢ postage and handling) payable to *Harlequin Reader Service*:

Harlequin Reader Service
Book Rack Offer
901 Fuhrmann Blvd.
P.O. Box 1396
Buffalo, NY 14269-1396

Offer not available in Canada.

BKR-1A

*New York and Iowa residents add appropriate sales tax.

It was a misunderstanding that could cost a young woman her
virtue, and a notorious rake his heart.

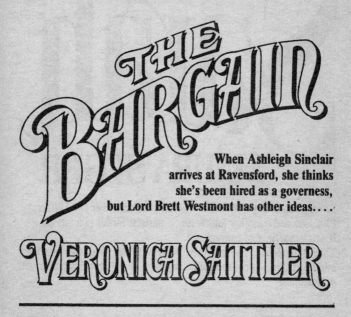

When Ashleigh Sinclair
arrives at Ravensford, she thinks
she's been hired as a governess,
but Lord Brett Westmont has other ideas....

VERONICA SATTLER

Sarah

MAURA SEGER

Sarah wanted desperately to escape the clutches of her cruel father.
Philip needed a mother for his son, a mistress for his plantation.
It was a marriage of convenience.
Then it happened. The love they had tried to deny suddenly became a
blissful reality... only to be challenged by life's hardships and brutal
misfortunes.
